THE SPRING RENEWS

THE SPRING RENEWS

MARIE MCGRATH

Other works by Marie McGrath

Novels

The Many Faces of Charlotte Barnes (My Book)

The Fall Changes

(My Book)

The Winter Heals

(My Book)

Anthologies

Christmas Magic (My Book)

For the latest news and updates, please check out Marie McGrath on her social media pages. Exclusive content and sneak peeks can be found in her FB Fan Page.

Twitter: @Marie_McGrath_

Instagram: marie_mcgrath_

Facebook: www.facebook.com/MarieMcGrathAuthor

Facebook Fan Page: www.facebook.com/groups/MarieMcGrathFans

Website:

https://mariemcgrathauthor.wixsite.com/books

ISBN: paperback 978-1-7353926-0-8
Library of Congress Control Number: 2021935283

Any references to historical events, real people or real places are used
fictitiously. Names, characters, and places are products of the author's
imagination.
Cover Design by Diana TC, triumphcovers.com
Edited by Brian Paone
Logo by Kevin Harless
First Printing Edition 2021
Published by Creative James Media

❀ Created with Vellum

To those going through grief, just remember, there is no right timeline

CHAPTER 1

*H*appiness oozed from every pore. Laughter echoed around the kitchen walls. My father sat next to me, while my brother was across the table. I didn't know what we were discussing anymore, but we just kept laughing, frozen in time.

"Sophie!" my mother screamed.

The shout startled me as I rolled from bed. My eyelids flitted closed, making it difficult to decipher the time as a yawn escaped from my mouth.

"You'll be late for school. Let's go already!"

And then it hit me. My stomach sank to my feet. *It was a dream.* I was once again the girl who had lost her father five —almost six—years ago. We weren't a group of four anymore. We weren't a unit. Instead, we had a piece missing —a piece I wasn't sure could ever be filled again.

"I'm up, Mama!" I shouted.

Nothing in my closet felt quite right for my mood today. Thanks to that lovely dream, I would rather sleep more or stay alone, but that wouldn't go well. I sighed and settled on a purple three-quarters-length sleeve shirt. I snatched jeans from the drawer and yanked them on. Rummaging through my sock drawer, I attempted to comb through the knots in my reddish-brown hair. It would have to be good enough.

I slammed the door to my purple bedroom, almost wishing something would fall to delay me further.

Smells of bacon wafted from the kitchen as I walked along the teal-covered hallway walls. I peered around the corner to watch Mama cook before I had to actually converse with anyone.

"What are you doing?" Caleb asked.

I sighed and rubbed my temples. It was too early to deal with little brothers. "None of your business."

He shrugged and walked around me.

Mama flipped an omelet in the skillet. She seemed so content. How were any of us content after losing Dad? He had been taken from us, and yet, it was like I was the only one who still cared. Was I the only one who still grieved his loss?

Mama turned and watched me. "Soph, there you are. You slept in. You need to go. I packed you something for lunch, and here's your omelet."

I walked toward her and kissed her cheek. "Thanks, Mama." The bag contained a sandwich—most likely a turkey one—apples, and some kind of salty goodness. Mama knew how to pack a lunch the way I liked it, which only let me slightly forgive her nonchalance when it came to Dad.

"Of course, I'll be home later than usual tonight. I signed up for some overtime. You and Caleb can order out. There's money in the jar for pizza."

"Score!" Caleb said with a mouthful of toast.

I rolled my eyes. "You're such a caveman."

"Am not!"

"Are too!"

"Enough," she said. "You two hurry up and eat. You don't have time to fight."

Caleb stuck out his tongue.

I aimed for his shin and smirked when his expression shifted into surprise and then pain. I shoved the last few bites of the omelet into my mouth, dropped the plate in the sink and grabbed the lunch off the counter. "Bye, Mama."

"Have a good day at school."

The door closed behind me. The warm air engulfed my body as I walked down the driveway. That dream lingered in my mind. This feeling needed to go away. How would I concentrate all day if all I felt was the rage of losing him in the navy?

My bag felt light as I shuffled it to my right shoulder. At least the sky was cloudless and the sun was bright. It finally felt like spring.

I yanked my earbuds from my bag and shoved them into my ears. My favorite playlist blared through them. I would never be able to finish the playlist before I found my way in front of the high school, but maybe a few of the songs would ease the tension that threatened to drag me down with it.

It had been a few months since I dreamt of my dad. Usually, I saw something the day before or heard a phrase that would remind me of him in order to dream, but I couldn't think of a single thing that would have triggered it. And that idea made me more nervous than anything. I had worked hard to not be triggered over the last few years, but if thoughts of him continued to rise to the surface, with no warning, I wasn't prepared for that.

God, how I missed him. Theodore James—or TJ to everyone but my brother and me—had been the best dad in the world. He might have been gone a lot with his job in the navy, but when he was home, he made us each feel so special. He would bring me little trinkets when he could or take me out without Caleb just for moments alone. Oh, how I missed those special moments with him. It was completely unfair that he had died serving this country. He had been due home soon when we got the word. It had been the worst summer of my entire life.

My brother didn't seem sad anymore, and Mama, while she hadn't moved on, I didn't catch her crying anymore. What was with them both? He had been the patriarch of our family, and they didn't seem bothered. It hadn't been his time to leave us, and no one seemed upset about it except me.

I huffed and focused on the road.

Let it go, Sophie. Let it go.

Honey Cove High loomed in the distance. I squinted as the sun angled perfectly into my gaze.

A horn honked in the distance and startled me over my music.

I raised my arm to my face and shielded my eyes, yanking one bud from my ear. It was Riley in her Impala.

"Get in!" she said.

I arched my eyebrow. "It's, like, fifty feet."

"So?"

"Okay." I plopped my bag on the floor and climbed in. "Thanks."

She nodded. "How was your weekend?"

"Boring. Caleb insisted on hogging the TV in the family room, and of course, Mama let him."

Riley giggled. "That's not awful. What'd he watch?"

"I don't even know. I stopped listening when I found out he wanted the TV."

"Gotcha. Well, you had the TV in your room."

I shrugged. "Yeah, but I wasn't in the mood, I guess." I stared out the window as she parked in the lot. "Let's go for a walk today. If you can, or is lover boy meeting you?"

Riley shot me a glance.

I giggled. "Randy. Sorry, just a habit."

"Mm-hmm. And no, he isn't. So, I'd be happy to go for a walk. But I need to stop at my house first. I didn't bring anything to run in."

I stared at her outfit as we got out. The flowy dress and ankle boots would make it difficult. "Dressing up for a certain someone?"

"No. I just felt like it would be nice to not wear pants today. I'm tired of the winter weather. I was hoping the weather would listen and be nice; it is the beginning of April after all."

I laughed. "If you say so."

My hand covered the smirk. She most definitely had dressed up for Randy. Why those two weren't officially dating yet was beyond me. I didn't know why she tolerated that. Well, that's not true. Randy doted on Riley like they were a couple. So, couple or not, she felt the attention from him.

If Randy wasn't who he was, I wouldn't have approved. He was probably the only guy in town who was good enough for her. No one else compared to the level of chivalry he displayed—at least toward her anyway. The rest of the guys in this town were helpless—too vain or too dorky. That was fine by me. I didn't need a boyfriend or a lover boy; they weren't worth the cost.

I linked arms with Riley. "You ready for today's foods class?"

She nodded. "I've been thinking about making crepes all morning. I just hope I don't screw it up."

"You and me both. Failing foods would be embarrassing."

Riley huffed. "Thanks for the reassurance, Sophie."

"Anytime."

"I'll catch you at lunch. Gotta run to my locker, and then I'm meeting Randy at his before English."

"See you later."

She continued straight down the hallway. Our lockers were as far apart as humanly possible, which sucked, but whatever. I would see her in a few classes anyway.

My hallway was deserted, except for one person halfway to my locker. I averted my gaze as Drew Abbott approached me.

Please don't see me. Please don't say anything.

I peeked at his appearance.

His black-framed glasses hung lopsided over his nose. As he readjusted them, his blond hair fell into his eyes. He met my gaze, and I quickly stared at the floor. "Hey, Sophie."

I glanced up. "Hey, Drew."

He stopped in front of me, blocking my way to my locker.

We stared at each other for what felt like thirty minutes, and then he moved on.

The knot in my stomach disentangled the farther away he got. Things were still strained between us. On some level, I could agree with how tragic it was that our friendship hadn't recovered from that barbecue, but I never knew what to say after I had learned he cared for me. I didn't want that. I wanted my friend. Jenna's dare had ensured we couldn't even be that anymore.

I shook my head. It was pointless to go down that road. Those thoughts were better for later … when I was alone.

~

The lunchroom was packed more than usual. I filtered through the people until I found our usual seats. It was funny to think how much had changed since the beginning of the year. I used to sit at this table by myself. Then Riley joined me, then Randy, and finally Shelby. It was surreal when I stopped to think about it.

Riley and Randy had already beat me there.

"No. I'm not doing it," Riley said.

I arched my eyebrow and stared at them both. "Do what?"

Riley met my gaze and huffed. "Randy is crazy. He wants me to stand in front of English class tomorrow to read my paper. He's lost his mind."

Randy sighed and combed his fingers through his hair. "I have not. I just want other people to hear your paper. It's so good. It should be shared."

I hid my smirk behind my lunch bag. If Riley saw me, I'd pay for it later when we went on a walk.

"Sophie, what do you think? Should I?"

I put both hands in front of me, palms out. "I'm not getting in-between you two. I know better."

Shelby sauntered over and placed her lunch tray on the table. "Between whom? What'd I miss?"

I still would have never imagined that Shelby Rowe—Honey Cove High's most popular girl in school—would ever sit at my lunch table, let alone every day. It was a new occurrence, but one I still had difficulty adjusting to. Shelby had always ignored me, which I supposed was better than being a target. But she had never been nice—at least, until Riley had arrived last fall to attend our school. It had puzzled me at first, but Shelby had stayed true to her word this January when she ditched her yes-girls. I expected a relapse on several occasions, but nothing ever happened. And honestly, I didn't mind her that much anymore.

"Those two are discussing if Riley should read her paper in English tomorrow."

Shelby's eyebrows rose. "Oh, yeah I agree with Sophie. Not touching that subject."

Riley crossed her arms and sighed. "You two are absolutely no help."

"We *are* helpful, but that's not a topic I'm broaching

between the two of you." Shelby smiled. "Now, if you want to discuss you two making things official, I'll discuss that."

Randy popped a fry into his mouth. "Is that so? What about you and Luke, Shelby? How goes that?"

Shelby's cheeks reddened. "We weren't discussing me."

I smirked. Their banter was frequent, and it never stopped being entertaining. They would circle each other a few more times before they all let it go. It was like siblings arguing. They meant well for each other but just couldn't help calling each other out.

Riley rolled her eyes. "Let's discuss something else, shall we? Why must our relationships always be a topic of conversation?"

"As the one painfully alone, I agree with this sentiment."

"I can set you up on a few dates," Shelby said.

"No! I didn't mean it like that. I'm perfectly fine being alone. But that doesn't mean I must be constantly aware of that fact every day."

"Fair enough," Riley added.

"So, you two ready to make some decadent crepes?" Randy asked between bites of his lunch.

"Ready as I'll ever be," Riley said.

"We'll do just fine. I practiced this weekend."

Riley reached across the table and pushed my bag. "You did? You didn't tell me that."

I shrugged. "Didn't think it was worth mentioning. Mrs. Pruitt won't make a big fuss about it. It's just foods class; as long as you try, you get an *A*. How hard can it really be?"

Riley gasped. "Don't say that! You'll jinx us."

Randy grasped Riley's hand and rubbed her palm with his thumb. "Breathe. Sophie's right; you'll do fine."

Shelby nodded. "Don't stress. Her class is a breeze. I had her last year, and she really does just check that you try."

Riley crossed her arms. "Says the girl who makes the best homemade red velvet cupcakes. I doubt you burned crepes!"

Shelby giggled. "Well, no. But that's not the point."

"Riley, you know it's an easy class. We've had her for a few months. Have you failed any projects yet?"

"No."

Randy held Riley's hand. "See? You'll be fine. And you should bring me one. Crepes are delicious." He winked at her as he released her hand.

I smiled as I watched them stare into each other's eyes. They were so cute together. It was hard not to be happy for them.

The lunch bell rang, signaling it was almost time to switch classes.

I stood and gathered my trash. "I guess it's time. You ready to go?"

Riley nodded. "I'll meet you there."

"Okay." I waved to Randy and Shelby. "See ya later."

They nodded and tidied their spaces.

I walked away as Randy waited for Riley. I didn't need to hang around while the lovebirds said goodbye. I meant what I had said; they were good for each other, but I didn't need to see it all the time. Plus, they needed their privacy, and I would see Riley in class and after school.

~

"I was so worried about my crepes that I didn't expect you to burn them!" Riley giggled.

I rolled my eyes. "Ha-ha. I'm over the joke."

We walked side by side toward Riley's Impala. All I wanted to do was take off into a sprint. Drowning out my thoughts with a playlist and running would help calm me down. This day just wasn't worth spending any more time on.

Riley touched my shoulder. "Sophie, you know I'm just messing with you. I'm sure Mrs. Pruitt will let you do it again. Just tell her you had a bad day. Make up a story, and she'll cave."

"Maybe."

Other students climbed into pickups and small cars. They all scurried to their vehicles to ditch the traffic leaving school. I never understood what the rush was. So what if you had to stay in the parking lot for a little longer? Where did any of us really have to go that we couldn't wait ten more minutes?

A hand waved in front of my face. "You in there? You seem like a serious space cadet," Riley said.

"I'm fine. Just trying to decide what to tell Mrs. Pruitt, and I really want to run."

Riley unlocked her Impala and tossed her bag in the back seat. "Gotcha. We'll get to my house soon, and then you can do just that. But you have to get in first."

I nodded. "Sorry. I'm just grouchy today."

Riley arched her eyebrow. "I noticed." She continued to eye me from the driver's seat.

I forced my gaze in the other direction and focused on the newly green grass that pervaded the scene. In a few days or so, the blooms would be out in full and populating the fields before they were planted. It was a wonderful time of the year. The air crackled with the warmth from the sun. The bite from the cold air was mostly absent except in the early morning or late evening hours. I usually loved the new freedom from the longer days and the warmer air—but this time, I couldn't help feeling bitter about everything.

Or maybe that was my dream talking.

I reached for Riley's radio and cranked up a country song. Before I knew it, we pulled into her long driveway.

"I'll get changed quick. You want to come in or wait out here?"

"I'll stretch out here." I inhaled the scent of the trees and the flowers from her mom-mom's garden. Over the last few months, I had become intimately acquainted with this home. I spent as much time at Riley's as I did at my own. It was nice to have another close friend.

When Jenna moved at the end of last school year, I lost touch with anyone my age who actually understood me. It had been a nice blessing when Riley moved from New York City.

I held my leg behind my back to stretch. When I counted to twenty, I switched legs. My arms and then back were the next things to stretch. By the time Riley returned, I was jogging in place, ready to run.

The sun ray's beat through my shirt and warmed me from the outside in. The sensations were ones I relished every change of season. There was nothing like freezing to death for months then being able to stand outside without a coat.

Riley jogged down the porch stairs to where I stood. "Ready to go?"

"Yep, all stretched. Don't you want to stretch?"

Riley scrunched her nose. "Afraid I'll pull something, or hoping to gain an advantage?"

I giggled. "You're crazy. It isn't even track season, which, by the way, be prepared for. I'll crush you this fall. But I genuinely just wanted to make sure you'd be okay."

Riley smirked. "I'll be fine. I stretched while I changed."

My eyebrows rose. "How … You know what? Never mind. I don't want to know how you managed that."

Riley burst into a fit of giggles. "Get your mind clear.

When I crush you in this run, I want it to be because you're focused."

I stopped jogging in place and eyed her. "Oh, I'm focused. You're on."

"Good. Don't inhale my dust too much. It's not good for you." Then she took off running.

No warning.

No countdown.

"Hey! That's cheating!" I yelled as she ran down her driveway. I shook my head and launched in her direction. She would be in so much trouble when I caught up with her.

CHAPTER 2

The sweat poured from my brow as I wiped it away with the back of my hand. I still trailed Riley, but she was admittedly much farther from me than I had hoped. It wasn't just her longer strides that edged her ahead. Her skill and talent had improved since first joining the track team several months ago.

Her winter conditioning and spring training for the fall kept her in shape. I was happy for her. I was, but, for whatever reason, the better she became, the worse I felt like I was. Maybe I just needed to focus. That was honestly probably my issue. My focus had tanked lately, and I didn't know what had happened.

I dug the ball of my foot into the ground and pushed myself to close the distance between us. She beat me because I wasn't trying. No one was to blame but me.

Riley's brunette ponytail swished back and forth behind her head. It mimicked the steady rhythm of her feet on the pavement. *Swish, swish. Swish, swish.*

I focused on the rhythm until I was right behind her.

Riley glanced back, hearing my feet slapping the

pavement behind her. "I was wondering what happened to you. You've been back there for a while."

"Yeah. Was paying more attention to the scenery than anything else."

"Do you want to slow down?"

"Not yet. Let's hit two miles first."

"That's right at the stop sign."

"Beat you there," I said then passed her.

Riley easily caught up with me but maintained that pace until we hit the stop sign.

We slowed until we were in a fast-paced walk.

"Thanks."

"Sure. It's a beautiful day. And I don't mind slowing down to look around."

"Maybe the weather will finally turn for good?"

"Hopefully. I'd be more than happy to have seventy-degree days for the rest of the year."

"Ha. Good luck with that. Enjoy this while it lasts. Soon the summer heat and humidity will scorch it all."

"Ugh. Don't remind me."

I swiped the back of my hand across my face. "We should have been more prepared. Nice day or not, it's stupid to run without water."

"Oh, well, we can make a stop at Morgan's."

"If we go that far, we might as well stop at my house."

"That's fine too."

"I can check on Caleb anyway. Mama won't be home for a while tonight. She's been so busy lately. I feel like I've barely seen her."

"Working a lot?"

I nodded. "That's what she says, anyway. I'm not sure why she keeps taking extra shifts though. It's not like we have any extra expenses lately. Unless she's saving up for a vacation or something big."

Riley gasped. "Oh, is she going to buy you a car?"

I wrinkled my nose. "I doubt it. She isn't into frivolous things. If I can walk there, why would I drive?"

"You can't walk *everywhere*, Sophie."

"I can too. I don't go anywhere besides school or your house. Morgan's is close enough to walk to, and anything else I might do, I go with you. And you drive, so I'm fine."

"If you say so. Then maybe you're right. Maybe she's planning to take you all on a summer vacation?"

"Maybe."

The rest of the way to my house, we stayed focused on our pace. Once we hit Main Street, we picked it back up in our final push.

My legs were in that post-workout jelly phase as I reached for the doorknob. It turned easily in my hand. I opened the door and listened for Caleb. "You home?" I shouted.

"In my room!"

I shook my head. "Little brothers are so dumb. He had the door unlocked. What if someone snuck in while he was in his room and got him?"

Riley smirked.

"What?"

"You're being a bit harsh; don't you think?"

I put my hands on my hips. "No. Someone could have robbed us. He's supposed to keep the doors locked if he's the only one home."

Riley crossed her arms. "Do you have your keys? Or are they still in your bag at my house?"

I bit the corner of my lip. "That's not relevant."

"Mm-hmm."

Caleb sauntered to the living room from the hallway. "You're home la—" His eyes widened, and he straightened his posture. "Oh, Riley. I didn't realize you were here too."

He smoothed his hair with his hands and straightened his shirt.

"Hi, Caleb."

I rolled my eyes. Caleb was ridiculous, always hitting on her or concocting excuses to be around Riley. And she thought it was endearing—cute even. *Bleck.* "Yes, Riley is here. Why don't you go do your homework?"

Caleb crossed his arms. "You aren't the boss of me. And besides, I'm already done."

"I am too the boss when Mama isn't home."

Caleb rolled his eyes. "I'm allowed to stay home by myself, which means you aren't the babysitter."

"Whatever. We aren't staying long. Grabbing some water bottles and running back to Riley's. Will you be fine here for a while?"

"Duh, Sophie. I'll play my videogames and order a pizza, like Mama suggested."

I squinted and glared. "Fine. I'll eat at Riley's then. Don't do anything stupid while I'm gone. And for all that is good and holy, *lock* the door, won't you?"

Caleb stuck out his tongue. "Yeah, yeah. Get your water and go. I'm fine."

I strolled past him and into the kitchen. I grabbed two water bottles and took a seat at the table. I sucked down the water while I surveyed the room.

It wasn't anywhere near as nice as Riley's house. Where they had white cabinets and marble countertops, we had black laminate counters and white-washed cabinets. Decades worth of wear and tear made it obvious on the hinges and handles. The doors hung crookedly, and handles felt loose when I grabbed them.

But even so, it was well loved, even if it was well worn. Mama had tried to update it over the years as much as possible—new paint here and there, the most recent a sort of gray-green color. Our appliances weren't stainless steel but black. And even though they all matched, they still didn't have the same gleam. Either way though, I never heard Riley say anything about it. And at least she didn't seem to care.

I fiddled with the lid to my bottle. "You don't care if I stick around for dinner at your house, do you?"

"Not at all. I would have suggested it anyway. Then I can drive you home afterward."

I smiled. "Thanks, Riley."

"Of course. That's what I'm here for. Friends are always there for each other."

"True. Let me grab an over-the-shoulder bag with a change of clothes. I don't want to sit at your mom-mom's table in these stinky clothes."

She giggled. "No worries. Then you'll be ready to go?"

"Yep."

I snatched a change of clothes—yoga pants and an oversized T-shirt—and stuffed them into my bag. I peered into my brother's room. He was playing his videogames with his headset on. I snuck in, grabbed a pillow and launched it at his head.

He whirled around and glared. "You almost made me *die.*"

"Oh, wah. You'll make it. I wanted to let you know we're leaving. Please lock the door, okay?"

He nodded.

"If you need me, just text me."

"I will, but I'll be fine." He plopped his headset back over his ears and tuned me out.

Riley waited by the door.

"All set."

We both left through the front door and started our pace. What better way to enjoy a spring day than a run with your best friend?

The shower was heavenly. After our run to Riley's house, sweat had been dripping from every surface of my body. My muscles were tender and stretched, but it was a feeling I enjoyed. It meant I had pushed myself, and in a sport where I had to count on myself more than others, that was what mattered.

I strolled down the hallway toward Riley's room. The door creaked, and I plopped on her bed next to her. "Whatcha doing?"

She smirked as she stared at her phone. "Nothing. Just texting Randy."

"Ah. Back from his sister's appointment?"

She nodded.

I watched her as she gripped her phone and smiled every time it vibrated in her hand. I didn't know what it was like to have a boyfriend. I didn't understand how one person could cause so much happiness, but I supposed it was possible. I mean, everyone always raved about it anyway.

"Are you happy?" I covered my mouth with my hand. I hadn't meant to ask that. Not out loud.

Riley looked up from her phone and met my gaze. "With Randy?"

I nodded.

She smiled, and her eyes took on this dreaminess, like the vision in front of her was of something I couldn't see but was magical. "I am. I know it seems crazy, since we aren't *together*, but I don't really need the title. I know he doesn't see anyone else the way he looks at me. And honestly, I feel like he treats me better than some girls' boyfriends do."

"That makes sense."

She patted my hand. "You'll find your guy someday."

I huffed. "Who says I want to?"

"You can fool a lot of people but not me, Sophie."

I crossed my arms. "What makes you think I'm even interested in that?"

"I can just tell. It's the glint in your eye when Shelby and Randy go on about me or Luke. It's subtle, but it's there." She scooted closer. "You have to open yourself up to options."

"Options? What options do I have?"

"You know, I bet a certain someone would be worth getting to know if you let him."

My eyes widened. "You can't mean …"

"Drew? Yes, I do."

"Why do you insist that something should happen between me and Drew? You don't even interact with him."

She shrugged. "I can't explain it. I just think he'd be perfect for you. Ever since you told me that story and we saw him at the theaters, I just felt the connection." She poked me in the side. "And the fact that you deny any involvement or feelings with him makes me think you, deep down, secretly wish it would happen."

My eyes widened. "You're crazy. Absolutely crazy pants. There is no way I would go out with Drew. We barely even speak anymore. We both avoid each other in the hallways at school. It makes no sense. He's not an option."

Riley smirked. "Whatever you say. I was just telling you my opinion."

I crossed my arms and puffed out my lip. "How did we even start discussing Drew?"

She giggled. "No idea." She rose from her bed and proffered a hand. "Ready to go downstairs? I think I smell food."

I grasped her hand and nodded. It would be a welcomed topic change; although, her comments swirled in my head. Drew would never forgive me for what had happened. Our friendship had been destroyed, and even if I wanted that part of it back, how could we deny his feelings from before? I had handled that whole situation badly.

No. There was no way anything would change between us. Things were irrevocably broken, and unless some divine intervention occurred, I couldn't imagine anything changing that fact.

CHAPTER 3

Saturday mornings were my absolute favorite day of the week. They promised relaxation, fun, and a chance at a new start. I couldn't explain how they managed to do all of that, but, for me, they did.

After my shower, I threw on jeans and a mint-green V-neck. I strolled down the hallway to the kitchen, smiling. My mood felt lighter than a few days before. That dream had messed with me. It took me back to that first month after he had died and the rage I had felt from his death.

The sounds of hushed voices lofted toward me as I turned the corner. I stopped dead and stared at the unfamiliar male sitting at our kitchen table. From behind, I could tell he had black hair, tanned skin, and wore a polo with pants that resembled the golf slacks men wore on TV.

Who was this man? And why was he in our kitchen?

Mama's petite figure rose from the chair across from him. Her eyes sparkled as she stared at his face. Her gaze rose to meet mine, and her jaw slackened and then recovered. "Sophie. You're up. Perfect timing."

I crossed my arms. "Perfect timing for what?" I narrowed

my gaze as the strange man turned in his seat and sized me up.

He proffered his hand and rose from his chair. "I'm Rowan Ashburn. It's nice to meet you. I'm a friend of your mom's. I've heard so much about you."

I crinkled my forehead and knitted my brows. "Oh? Because I've heard nothing about you."

Caleb bounded from behind me. "Hey, Row! How's it going?"

I watched as they high fived each other.

How did Caleb know him?

I balled my fists. "Somebody better explain this now. *How are you friends? And, Caleb, how do you know him?*"

Mama stepped toward me. "Sophie, why don't you sit for breakfast, and we can talk about it."

Reluctantly, I listened. I studied this man's features like I might have to explain it to a detective. His eyes resembled the golden tones of honey, and freckles covered his nose but barely on his cheeks. Creases circled his eyes and lined his forehead, like he squinted too frequently.

Caleb smiled at him. "So, Row, how was your last tee time?"

"It was great. I birdied most of the holes and had par for the rest of them."

"That's awesome."

Rowan turned and faced me. "Sophie, your mom tells me you like to run."

I nodded.

She nudged my shoulder and placed a plate in front of me. "Why don't you tell him what events you run for track?"

"Sprints and relays."

She glared at me. "Sophie is being humble. She's one of the best track runners on her team."

"That's fantastic. I was never a runner. I could swing anything and make it go far, but running was a no go."

Of course, it was. Who was this guy? Why did he want to *bond* with me?

"Sophie *was* the best player until Riley showed up. That girl crushes her on the track," Caleb said as he shoved a handful of toast into his mouth.

I glared at him. "Shut it, dweeb."

"Hey, none of that. It's too early," Mama said.

Rowan chuckled.

Did we amuse him? Did he think we were funny? Ugh, this guy was terrible, and I wanted him out of this house … as soon as I figured out what he was doing here to begin with.

I glared at him while he sipped on a glass of orange juice. "Why are you here?"

He choked on the juice and pounded his chest with a closed fist. "I … uh."

"Sophie Rene Graham! You have better manners than this."

I slumped in my chair. So what if she was right? I wanted answers, and everyone was keen on making this long and drawn out. So much for my Saturday being a new start.

"Sorry," I mumbled.

He nodded.

Mama placed several platters on the table: eggs, bacon, and sausage links. A plate of toast and assorted jams also adorned the table.

I piled the food onto my plate and shoved forkful after forkful into my mouth. If I couldn't talk, I couldn't say anything that would get me in more trouble.

Mama stared, jaw slackened, as I forced in the food.

Maybe I needed to rethink my strategy?

The napkin by my plate was rumpled. I smoothed it out

then placed it on my lap. I straightened my posture and watched as Rowan ate his breakfast. The table was silent.

Through clenched teeth, I asked, "So, Rowan, what do you do for a living?"

"I'm head of marketing for Rowe Industries."

I grimaced. Of course, he worked where she did. But how would she have ever met him?

I watched Mama ogle at him from across the table. What was happening? She was acting like a lovesick—

Oh no! He couldn't … They couldn't.

I elbowed her. "Can we talk for a second?"

She eyed me warily then nodded. "Excuse us for one moment."

I watched Caleb and Rowan as I waited for her to join me in the hallway. Caleb was relaxed and comfortable with this man. How long had he known him? Known of him?

Mama crossed her arms. "What is it, Sophie? I don't want to be rude to our guest."

I stared into Mama's green eyes that resembled mine. "Who is Rowan to you?"

"What?"

"Who is *he* to *you*?"

"He's a coworker."

I rolled my eyes. "A coworker? He said friend, but you're making googling eyes at him like a lovestruck teenager. Who is he?"

I pleaded with my heart to be wrong. I begged the words that came next to not be what I thought.

"He … We're dating."

My heart slammed against the walls of my chest. The thundering rebounded in my ears, and my face flushed. *"Dating?* You can't be serious. Aren't there rules about dating someone from work? What were you thinking?"

"Excuse me, but I'm the parent, and you're the child. You

do not have the right to scold me about what I do with my personal life."

"Your personal life? If you're dating him, he's *involved* with us all!"

Her gaze narrowed. "I wanted this to be a nice breakfast, then maybe we could take a stroll through town, possibly do something as a family, but you're being awful to him and to me." She reached for my arm. "What's going on with you lately?"

The tears welled, and my throat burned as the thoughts and realizations crashed over me. How could she be dating? How could she have moved on? "If you wanted this to be a good breakfast, maybe you shouldn't have let a random stranger appear at the table. You should've given me a warning." I clawed at the dampness around my eyes. "I didn't expect you to move on so fast."

"So fast? Sophie, it's been almost six years since your father died."

"So?"

Mama sighed and tossed her red hair over her shoulder. "Can you please rejoin us? We can discuss this more later."

I shuffled my feet. "How does Caleb already know him? You told him and not me?"

"It wasn't on purpose, Sophie. Your brother was home when Rowan dropped me off a few times. I had to tell him."

"And you didn't tell me once I got home? They're buds already, and I'm left in the dark. That really sucks, Mama."

"I'm sorry, Sophie. I didn't know how to tell you, and it hasn't been that long since he knew."

I crossed my arms. "Fine."

How could she not see how hurtful that was? My dweeb of a brother knew before I did, and yet, she shrugged it off like it wasn't a big deal, like moving on after my father wasn't a big deal. I still had nightmares and dreams about him.

Sometimes in the garage, it was like he was with me. I would hear his voice when I didn't know what to do. I would feel his embrace when I was sad.

Mama pulled me close and walked with her arm over my shoulder back toward the table.

I sat and smiled weakly at Rowan. The food on my plate was no longer appetizing, so I pushed it around with my fork and took a bite here and there. I would dutifully sit and listen, but I couldn't be expected to do much more.

"How was school this week, Caleb?" Rowan asked.

He slumped in his chair. "I had a big history test. I don't know if I did well or not. Mr. Avis is hard to listen to. His voice is so monotone, and he just tells these stories all class."

Rowan chuckled. "History teachers can be like that, but I always found the stories were generally the lessons."

Caleb shrugged. "Maybe."

"You didn't tell me you had a test, Caleb. I would have helped you," Mama said.

"You were busy. It's fine."

Mama pursed her lips.

No one ever asked if I had tests. I had studied by myself for as long as I could remember. Then again, Caleb and I were always different that way. While I didn't have straight As, school seemed easier for me than for him.

The scents of the bacon and sausage turned my stomach. Their smells usually intoxicated me, but today, my stomach felt as if nothing would stay down now.

"Can I go golfing with you sometime?" Caleb asked.

I glared. Why was he not as upset about this as I was? Sure, he was younger, but did he not realize he erased his father's memory every time he got closer to this man? This stranger?

Rowan smiled. "Sure, if your mom says it's okay."

Mama nodded. "I think that's a great idea."

I rolled my eyes. Of course, she did; encourage him to move right in, why didn't she?

A swift kick to the shin startled me. I rubbed my shin as I scanned the table. Who had kicked me?

Caleb seemed oblivious, but Mama stared me down. Had she seen me roll my eyes?

"Sophie, would you want to come?"

"No."

Another kick.

"Uh … I mean, no thank you. I don't like golf."

"Ah. I understand. Too stuffy for a nice young lady like yourself. Maybe we could all do something else? With the weather getting nicer, maybe we could do some miniature golf?"

"That's a wonderful idea," Mama said.

"Oh, or what about the spring festival?" Caleb offered.

I groaned. I didn't want to get stuck with this man at the festival. I already had plans to go with Riley, Randy, and Shelby. I didn't want a parental escort.

"Sounds great." Rowan eyed me, keeping his posture open and his eyes as if they were smiling.

Our guidance counselor had given us a lesson about body language for our school interviews next year, and, if I remembered correctly, open posture was supposed to be welcoming. Well, his welcoming stance could shove it. I didn't want him to welcome me into whatever this was.

"How long have you two been dating?" I asked.

Mama's jaw slackened. "Sophie!"

Rowan waved her off. "It's okay, Faye. I don't mind." He faced me. "Today is six months."

"*Six months?* Six months!"

"Sophie, calm down."

My chair wobbled with the force from my body as I scooted backward. "You've been dating for half a year, and you just now say something. This is ridiculous." I threw my napkin on the table and ran to my room. I grabbed my house key and phone and bolted out the front door.

I faintly heard my name, but I refused to turn around and look. The sky was blue, with large puffy clouds—the complete opposite ambience to my mood. I wanted thunderheads and lightning streaking the sky. I wanted earthquakes and tornadoes ripping apart homes. Because then, just maybe, the rage that boiled beneath my skin wouldn't surface.

At the end of the neighborhood was a medium-sized playground. I strolled to the swings and plopped onto the middle one. I pushed hard off the ground and tucked my legs underneath. I closed my eyes and let the breeze collide with my face with each swing. The coolness and the movement lessened my rage—but only slightly.

I pulled up my messages and clicked on Riley's name. *My mama is DATING someone. In fact, has been for six months!*

The swing slowed. I tapped my feet on the tire chips as I waited for a response. *Come on, Riley. Answer me!*

The chirp startled me before I swiped to unlock my phone.

What? Are you serious?

YES! She told me this morning. Oh, and the best part is Caleb already knew. No idea for how long, but he knew. What was she thinking, Riley? I've never been so angry in my whole life.

I'm sorry. How did you find out?

The guy sat at our kitchen table this morning. He was already there when I walked around the corner. Can you believe that?

Wow. Not the best introduction.

He might be a nice guy, but we don't need anyone else in our family. We're doing just fine.

What are you going to do?

I don't know.

I started swinging again—back and forth, back and forth. I tried to release my anger. I tried to release it all, but my arms and legs tingled with the intensity of my clenching.

I have an idea, but I'll need your help to make it work.

Whatever you need. I'm always here.

Can you come by?

Sure. Be there in thirty.

You're the best!

I shoved my phone in my back pocket and strolled to the house. I would have just enough time to get changed, hopefully avoid Mama, and bolt from the house.

I folded my arms and surveyed the homes I passed. Most yards were empty even though it was on the warmer side today. The Jadwins were outside in their back yard around the flowerbeds. They probably were weeding before the beds got out of control with warmer days ahead.

And then I saw him. Drew stood in front of his bedroom window, oblivious to my presence outside his house. I quickened my speed to ensure he didn't see me. I didn't need any more drama, especially not with boys.

If anything, this whole ordeal with Mama had solidified how wrong love was. I didn't need it. And I didn't want it.

CHAPTER 4

"Thank you so much for rescuing me," I said.

"No problem." Riley eyed my outfit. "What are you wearing?"

I looked down at my khaki pants and a nice red blouse. "It's part of the plan."

She cocked her head. "Care to explain?"

"I'm going to get a parttime job."

"What?"

"Yep. A job."

She scrunched her eyebrows. "I'm not following how a job will help you avoid your mom dating someone? Or deal with that situation at all."

"I can't see it if I'm not home."

"So, you're getting a job?"

"Yes!"

"Sophie, that makes no sense."

I frowned. "Of course, it does. She can't make me stay home from a job. She could use help, and she knows it. If I spent time at your house or something, it wouldn't work. She would ground me or something. This plan is foolproof."

Riley chuckled. "I don't know if I would say it's foolproof. Do you even want to work somewhere?"

I shrugged. "Sure. It won't be that bad."

"How will you get there?"

I hadn't thought about that. I didn't have a car, so that could present a problem. "I don't know. I'll figure it out if I get something."

Riley stifled giggles. "Yep. Totally foolproof."

"Whatever."

"Well, where can I drive you, madam?"

I rolled my eyes. "Anywhere you think would hire me."

"Uh? Any suggestions. I don't know where you want to work."

I pointed to the side street. "Start at Morgan's. Maybe Randy can help me out."

She nodded and pulled into the parking lot.

"Is he working today?"

"I think so."

"Good. I'll be just a minute."

Riley's hand froze on her seatbelt. "You don't want me to come in with you?"

"Nope. I need to do this one myself."

"Okay." She reclined in her seat and turned the radio louder.

I climbed from the Impala and smoothed out my outfit. It wasn't formal, but it was nicer than what I had worn earlier. If an employer couldn't handle this, did I want to work there? I wasn't so sure.

The automatic doors opened as I stepped on the mats in front of the doors. The cool breeze from the air condition hit me, and I shivered. It wasn't hot enough for full-blown air condition, but I wouldn't hold it against Morgan's Market.

I surveyed the floor for Randy. He stocked the shelves, so he could either be on the salesfloor or in the back, getting more packages. I found him by the deli counter, his cart full of buns, rolls, and other types of bread. I strolled up next to him and patted his shoulder. "Hey, Randy."

He faced me and smiled. "Hey." He looked around me. "Alone today?"

"Riley's in the car."

Randy's smile faltered slightly. "Oh."

"She wanted to come in; don't worry."

His expression brightened. "Ah, so what's up?"

I twisted my blouse around my fingers. "I was wondering if you knew of any job openings here."

He stroked his chin. "I don't think so. We just hired two new cashiers. Everyone else has been here awhile."

I sighed. "Darn it."

"But I'll keep an eye out and let you know if I hear anything."

"Okay. Thanks, Randy."

"Of course. Can you say hello to Riley for me? Let her know I'll text her back later?"

I nodded. "Catch you later." I turned and walked away. Strike one.

Riley twirled her long brunette hair around her finger when I returned.

I smirked. She was nervous. "Lover boy said hello, and he'll text you later."

"What? How?"

I eyed her warily. "Don't pretend you weren't worried about what happened in there and what he was doing."

"I-I wasn't."

"Mm-hmm. Your hair wasn't curly enough?"

She dropped the strand of hair. "No fair."

I giggled. "Well, he was sad you didn't come in too. But, before you get all worked up, I told him it was my idea."

She rolled her eyes. "Well, thank you. I suppose."

"You're welcome."

"So? Any luck?"

"Nope. We must keep trying."

She put the car in Reverse and backed from the parking spot. We accelerated on the main road and continued our search. It couldn't take too long, right?

~

*I*n fact, it *could* take forever. I underestimated how difficult it was for a high schooler to get a job. Even in a small town with lax rules on starting ages, there were less opportunities. Which is how I now relied on the movie theater from the next town over to hire me. It was my last resort.

"I'll check it out. Wait for me?" I asked.

Riley nodded. "Of course. Good luck."

I slammed the Impala door and watched as Riley drove into the parking lot. This was my only hope; it had to work. If I was stuck at home with Mama and her boyfriend, I would die. Absolutely dissolve into dust.

The door swung back behind me as I crossed the threshold. It was late in the afternoon, and a fair crowd had already formed at the snack counter and in the lounge area. The dark purple walls sucked all the outside light from the room, and the blue carpet made unvacuumed crumbs more obvious.

I scanned the floor for an employee—someone in charge, not just anyone.

In the corner behind the snack counter was a middle-aged man with salt and pepper hair and he had a serious expression, looking like a person in charge.

Straightening my spine, I sauntered toward the man and

tried to project confidence. Did I say this was my last chance? I cleared my throat. "Excuse me, sir."

The middle-aged man scowled. "Don't cut in line. If you need refreshments, line up like everyone else."

I followed the man's gaze and stared at the line.

A few people had noticed me, but several groups were focused on their phones.

"I-I'm not here for snacks. I was hoping I could submit an application."

The man scrutinized me and moved from behind the counter. He scrunched his nose. "Application? You want a job?"

I nodded.

"Follow me."

I weaved in and out of customers in line for snacks until we were in a back room with a small desk shoved in the corner and props and cardboard cutouts stacked high. Apparently, this theater believed in hoarding their advertisements.

The man pushed a small beat-up wheely chair toward me.

I sat and waited for him to speak.

"Any job experience?"

I shook my head. "Not officially, but I've babysat before."

The man stroked his chin. "How old are you?"

"Seventeen."

"I assume this would be for a few hours every week after school and on weekends?"

I nodded.

"We don't *need* anyone necessarily, but a floater is a great asset to any theater. Would you be willing to learn several positions?"

"I'd do anything."

"I don't usually hire just anyone off the street, but I like your drive, so here's what we'll do. I'll try you out on a few shifts and see how you do. If you pick it up, you can stay on. If not, I'll let you loose, and we'll go our separate ways. Deal?"

"If you don't mind me asking, I have two questions."

The man's eyebrows rose.

"What positions would I be learning? And how much would I make?"

"You'll train as floor staff, and that entails several duties. For example, the ticket booth, making and serving snacks, and usher-type duties. Pay is minimum wage."

"I'll do it."

The man smiled and stood. "What's your name?"

"Sophie Graham."

He proffered his hand across the desk. "Nice to meet you, Sophie. I'm Mr. Martin, theater manager. I'll be your head boss, but you'll shadow someone. I'll introduce you to them on your first shift. Can you start Tuesday at five?"

I shook his hand. "Yes, sir. I'll be here."

"Make sure to wear black pants and black shoes. No sneakers. Your shirt should be purple or black and no T-shirts. I'll see you at five."

"Thank you again."

He nodded and sat.

I assumed that meant it was time to leave. I hustled down the hallway and outside. My smile never wavered as I jumped into Riley's Impala a few rows back.

"And?"

I turned to face her. "I got a job!"

Riley smiled and high fived me. "Nice work! When do you start?"

"Tuesday at five." I batted my lashes. "Can you drop me off here at five?"

Riley smirked. "Yes. Now you only have to tell your mom."

I shivered. "Don't remind me!"

~

*R*iley drove me straight home, but the closer we got to my house, the more nervous I became. Mama would be mad. I had left when she wanted to talk and had avoided the house all day.

"Text me if you aren't dead," Riley said.

I nodded and climbed from the Impala. Maybe if I snuck in and pretended I was home, it wouldn't be so bad. The front door was unlocked. I slowly crept in and shut the door, careful to avoid making noise. I tiptoed around the gray sofa and toward the hallway.

"Sophie Rene!" Mama shouted. "Get in this kitchen, now!"

I hunched my shoulders. First and middle names always meant I was in deep trouble. I turned the corner to see Mama sitting at the table, arms folded. She glared as I sat. "Where have you been? You stormed out, left without telling me anything and come back hours later. Have you lost your mind?"

I gulped. "I'm sorry."

Her eyes narrowed. "That's it? You're sorry? Where have you been?"

"First, I walked to the little playground, then had Riley pick me up."

"And you couldn't have texted me to let me know? I was worried."

"I-I'm sorry, Mama. But I have good news."

Her left eyebrow arched. "About what? That you won't be rude to guests again?"

I squirmed. "Well, no. The news isn't about guests."

Mama scowled.

"I, well … I got a job."

Mama's jaw slackened. "You, what? Where?"

"The theater."

"How on earth will you get there? You don't have a car."

"I know. I don't work all the time. I start Tuesday. Riley will drive me."

Mama laid her head in her hands and rubbed her forehead. "Sophie, I don't even know what to do with you. A job? And then the stunt you pulled with Rowan? I just don't understand."

I didn't know if I was supposed to respond or not, so instead, I stayed perfectly still and silent.

Mama stood. "You embarrassed me today. Go to your room. I need to think about all of this."

I stood and practically sprinted from the kitchen. I had never seen her so upset; she had forgot to really yell at me. I had done the right thing, hadn't I? She would come around, and maybe she would even be happy about it, eventually.

CHAPTER 5

"Are you ready for your first shift tonight?" Riley asked and took a bite of her sandwich.

"I don't know if excited is the word. Mama is still barely talking to me."

Shelby's eyebrows rose. "Because you got a job? Shouldn't she be happy you'll be helping?"

"Not really. She has it all wrapped up into the thing with Rowan. So, I'm in deep."

"For what it's worth, Rowan is a very nice employee."

I grimaced. "He can be nice all he wants. It just doesn't have to be with my family."

Shelby shrugged.

I studied Riley's and Randy's expressions. Randy had been quiet, which was unusual for a conversation like this. "Randy, what do you think?"

Randy shifted in his chair. "I think I hope you have a good first shift."

I rolled my eyes. Typical. Staying out of it was probably easier than telling me what he thought. But I had a right to be angry about the arrangement. Mama should have never sprung it on me.

Shelby scooted closer. "Any idea what they'll have you do?"

"All I know is they want to train me for a few positions and I'll have to shadow someone. If I pick it up, I might have a job for the future; if I don't, he'll let me loose."

"That sounds pretty standard," Randy said. "When we get high school employees at Morgan's, we generally give them a trial period. It saves us from having to put up with someone who is terrible and should be let go."

"Well, I'll do whatever it takes to avoid the house. I'll be the best employee ever."

Riley snorted. "That's not usually the normal motivation for a job."

"Since when do I do anything the normal way?"

"Fair point."

"Well, I think it's resourceful. At least it's a job and not another hobby to stay away from your house," Shelby said.

I shrugged. "It's the easiest way to get Mama to agree. No other activity would have gotten me out of events like a job would."

Shelby tapped her chin. "I could have gotten you to *work* for us. Might have saved you."

My eyes widened. "Work for you? As in at Rowe Industries? I don't think I'd want to be at the same place as Mama and Rowan. That sounds terrible."

Shelby shook her head. "I mean me, like, with the festivals. Almost as an assistant. You wouldn't have to tell your mom you really answer to me."

"That sounds riskier, and besides, they're already giving me the chance. Who knows, it might be fun." I gulped down my bite of food. One could only hope that would be the truth.

"I don't think I'm ready for this," I said as I surveyed the theater from the passenger seat.

Riley patted my leg. "You've got this. Stop worrying."

My throat felt closed as I tried to swallow. "I don't know. What if I suck or they hate me?"

"Sophie, get real. You'll be fine." She checked the time. "But you must get out, or you'll be late. Do I need to get you later?"

"No. Mama wanted to pick me up. So, you're off the hook."

"Okey-doke. Now get out," she said and nudged me.

I swung the door open, hopped out and waved goodbye. One deep breath and I shoved open the entrance to the theater. It took a few moments for my eyes to adjust. The smell of popcorn invaded my senses. I scanned the lobby for Mr. Martin.

Our gazes met from across the lobby, and I sauntered in his direction.

"Sophie, welcome," he said.

"Mr. Martin, thank you again for this opportunity."

He raised his hand, palm out, stopping me like a crossing guard. "Remember, this is a trial basis. Don't thank me yet, just show me what you can do."

"Yes, sir."

He nodded. "Follow me. It'll be easier to discuss your shift in my office."

I followed him to the office where he had interviewed me. It was still cramped and crammed with movie posters. In fact, it seemed worse from just a few days ago.

Mr. Martin pointed to the chair in front of his desk, and I sat.

"Much better. Now, you'll shadow one of my employees

to learn the ropes. If you pass my inspections and this employee's evaluation of your work, I'll hire you on. Still okay with this deal?"

I nodded just as a knock sounded from the closed office door.

Mr. Martin rose. "Ah, here he is now. Come in."

I rose and turned to face the employee who would determine my fate. At the sight of the shaggy blond hair and dark-rimmed glasses, I nearly fainted. It couldn't be.

"Mr. Martin, Courtney said you needed me?" Drew asked.

"Drew, yes. I want you to meet Sophie. She'll be shadowing you for a few weeks. Sophie, Drew is one of the best. He'll show you the ropes."

I was speechless. My mouth felt like a desert, and words would no longer form. I found the tiniest crack in the wall to stare at, memorizing every detail and defect. What would he think? I managed to raise my chin and look above Drew's head to the hallway outside. "Um … hey, Drew."

Drew stared at me then at Mr. Martin. "The new employee is Sophie?"

Mr. Martin's eyebrows knitted together. "Yes. Is there a problem?"

"N-No, not at all," I answered for him and shook Mr. Martin's hand. "Thank you again. Drew, I'm ready to learn when you are."

He adjusted his glasses farther up on his nose and left the office.

I had to jog to catch up to him.

He turned swiftly. "Sophie, this is a bad idea."

"Drew, I need this. Please. I'll do whatever you say. Please, don't give up on me."

He sighed. "Okay, but I'm not your friend here." He coughed. "Well, you know what I mean. I won't go easy just because of our pasts. I take the theater seriously."

I raised both hands in defense. "I understand. Honestly, I didn't know I'd be shadowing you. We can pretend we don't know each other if that helps."

He scoffed. "You mean like we do at school and any other day?"

"I …" I nodded and hung my head.

He rolled his eyes and walked toward the lobby. He didn't seem like he wanted to be anywhere near me, but I had to shadow him, so I followed. He stopped at the podium to check tickets. The podium stood to the left side of the snack counter, allowing patrons to get their snacks immediately after entering.

"We'll start here. It's the easiest job in the theater as a floater. You're least likely to screw it up."

"Oh, thanks for the vote of confidence."

"It is what it is, Sophie. So, people can show us their tickets three different ways. The first is the paper stubs. You rip off one section and shove it in the slot then hand them their part back. For the other two types, you need this handheld scanner their phone or their paper that says they bought them digitally."

"Okay. Is there a code to use the handheld?"

"No. Just push the on button and go." Drew pointed to the older couple who strode toward us. "I'll show you what to do with them, then you can try on the next guest. If you manage to not mess it up, I'll leave you alone for a few. Deal?"

I nodded and watched to see what he would do. It wasn't like calculus; it couldn't be that hard.

"Good evening," Drew said as he ripped their paper tickets. "Theater ten is on your left, last door on the right. Enjoy your movie."

The couple smiled and walked toward their theater room.

"You greet them, take care of their tickets then direct them which way to go. Theater rooms one to five are on their right, six to ten are on their left." He pointed to a small sign on the podium. "This will help you remember until it comes naturally."

"Thanks."

"Sure. Okay, these two girls are yours. Remember: greet, tickets, direct."

"Got it." I smiled as the two younger teenagers approached the podium.

The taller girl outstretched her arm to present a code on her cellphone.

I grabbed the scanner and hit On. I scanned it, hoping it was correct, and waited for the beep on the screen. A green light pulsed at the top, which I assumed meant it had worked. I checked the theater number and smiled. "Good evening. Your theater is on your right, first door to the left."

The girls nodded and strolled to the theater door with their popcorn.

I spied Drew off to the side. "How did I do?"

"Not bad. Remember to greet as they approach, but nice work with the scanner. You did well for not seeing how it was used. Take the next couple and we'll see how you do."

I nodded and looked ahead, waiting for someone to approach the podium. I'd rather be busy learning or with guests than waiting. Down time reminded me of what had happened with Drew. It always lurked between us. How could I even apologize for embarrassing him and exploiting his feelings for me? Sure, I didn't come up with the dare, but he had tried to kiss me and kissed a dog instead. I couldn't imagine that happening to me. I would never forgive anyone.

I inhaled deeply at the sight of more couples approaching the podium. If I did these well, he would let me work on my own, and I could have some space. I needed this before the guilt drowned me.

"Good evening. Theater five is the last door on your right. Enjoy your movie," I said with a smile.

I cruised through the line quickly, remembering the three steps: greet, tickets, direct. I only hoped Drew agreed that I had done well.

Drew stroked his chin as he watched me. "Not bad, Sophie. I think you can manage it." He walked to the left and quickly returned with a headset. "You'll wear this when you're left alone on your shifts. Use it if you get over your head or you have questions. Nothing is too stupid to ask. I'd rather you ask than guess. Make sense?"

I put the earbud in my ear and clipped the rest of the headset to my shirt. "Absolutely."

Drew checked around the podium once more then walked away.

I had never been more thankful to be left alone in my life.

~

The end of my shift arrived slowly. On the one hand, I was proud of myself for going out of my comfort zone and getting a job. On the other hand, I wish I could have shadowed anyone else besides Drew. He seemed like a nice boss, but our history was so awkward, and I didn't know if I was the only one who still felt it.

I waited by the curb for Mama and opened up my messages. Riley would absolutely lose her mind when I told her who I had to shadow. I found our thread and texted her, *So, I have to shadow someone at work as part of my trial period and guess who it is.*

Shut up! Is it Drew?

That was a good guess. How'd you go straight to that?

Well, considering I don't know that many people who you know at that theater, I figured Drew would give you the most heartburn to shadow.

True.

So how was it?

I'll tell you later. Too much to text.

Mama pulled up to the curb just as Drew walked from the doors. Mama rolled down the window. "Drew? Drew Abbott, is that you?"

Oh crap. Why couldn't she have arrived sooner?

Drew strolled to the car window. "Hi, Mrs. Graham."

"It's so nice to see you, Drew. It's been a long time."

He nodded. "Yes. It was good to see you. I should get home."

"Of course. Have a good night, Drew."

He waved and walked into the parking lot.

I climbed into the passenger seat of Mama's SUV.

"What a wonderful surprise. Drew is such a nice young man. How come he doesn't come by anymore?"

I shrugged.

"Well, what a nice treat. I remember when you, Drew, and Jenna would be in the back yard for hours. I feel better knowing that Drew works here too. At least I'll know someone is here who can look out for you."

Was she serious? Drew was the furthest person from looking out for me. I wouldn't be surprised if he did the opposite.

Mama reached across the console to my knee. "So, how was it? I may not be happy with how you ended up with a job, but I am excited to hear how it went."

I sighed. "It was good. I'm on a trial basis, so I must shadow until they decide I'm a good fit. I worked at the ticket podium. It wasn't bad, and it's funny to see who went to what kind of movie. There were some that I didn't expect."

"Oh? Like what?"

"This one elderly couple went and saw the newest raunchy comedy, and another middle-aged couple went to see the new teen bop kind of movie. Was really strange."

Mama giggled. "Sounds like you had a good time."

"It'll do."

"I'm glad to hear that. When is your next shift?"

"They want me to work on Friday. The shift is five to ten."

"I should be home to pick you up. Can you get someone to drop you off?"

"Yeah, Riley won't mind."

"Perfect. Let's head home."

I nodded and watched out the window as she pulled away from the theater. One shift down, who knew how many more to go.

CHAPTER 6

I strolled to my lunch table and was happy to find everyone already seated. I needed their advice in how to deal with the Drew situation.

As I sat, I listened to Randy talk. "I'm just saying you could go a little easier and it would still be successful."

I scrunched my nose. "What are we talking about?"

Randy sighed and ran his hands through his hair. "Shelby at the next council meeting. She wants to go in there guns blazing, and I don't think that will exactly work."

Shelby frowned. "Those men are stubborn and big bullies. They don't want to listen, and we know we're right. Why can't they just accept it? Mr. Tate gets on my last nerve."

Randy chuckled. "Obviously. That's why he does it. Don't you think if he had no reaction he would chill out? He likes to purposely irritate everyone. Where do you think Priscilla gets all that? He'll come around when the rest of the founding council members agree to our edits to the proposal. You just need to act less emotionally attached."

Shelby rolled her eyes. "Less emotionally attached? What are they, allergic to passion?"

Riley giggled as she pushed her salad around her plate.

"No, but you know how they feel about females in charge. I don't think it's right, but ultimately, we don't want to kill any progress we've made with them by going in and being ridiculous. You need this to work still, or your mother will renege on the deal."

Shelby crossed her arms. "I hate when you're right."

Randy smirked. "I have good ideas here and there."

"Wow. What a scintillating conversation," I said. "Now, I have a different topic we need to discuss. I don't know what to do."

Riley straightened her posture. "Ooh, is this about last night?"

I nodded.

"What happened last night?" Shelby asked.

"I had my first shift at the theater."

"Did you forget to butter someone's popcorn?" Randy asked then smirked.

I sneered at him. "No. I have to shadow someone as part of my trial with the theater, and well, it's Drew. I shadow Drew."

Shelby and Randy exchanged glances, clearly unaware of how serious this was.

Shelby stabbed a piece of chicken with her fork. "So?"

"So, I humiliated him, and we barely talk anymore. What am I going to do?"

Shelby's eyebrow rose. "Humiliated him? The perfect Sophie did something bad?"

Riley giggled. "Oh yeah, she did. You should really tell them the story."

I glared at her. I had hoped I could avoid sharing every detail, but the way Shelby ogled me and Randy sat there, I knew I couldn't get out of it. "Fine. I was younger, so no judging."

"Do I want to hear this?" Randy asked.

Riley met his gaze. "Yes, you do."

Randy nodded and waited.

I sighed and closed my eyes. If I had to tell the story, I didn't have to look them in the eyes. "Drew lives in my neighborhood and so did Jenna. Do you remember her?" I peeked to see their response.

Shelby tilted her head sideways. "Did she have blond hair?"

I nodded.

"I think so."

Randy shrugged.

I squeezed my eyes shut again. "Anyway, we all spent time together at the barbecues in our neighborhood. We were all the closest in age compared to the other families, so we always gravitated to each other. Jenna liked to play truth or dare, and we suspected Drew had feelings for me. She was devious with her questions and her dares, but we still played. It was Drew's turn, and by surprise, he chose dare." I inhaled deeply then exhaled. "His dare was to kiss me."

Shelby clapped her hands together. "Ooh, I love it!"

Randy grimaced, while Riley smiled devilishly.

"Jenna thought it would be a good idea to instead have him kiss her dog when he went to kiss me. He leaned forward and shut his eyes, and, at the last minute, Jenna swapped my lips for her dog's. He kissed her dog, and when he opened his eyes, his face reddened, and Jenna cackled. I didn't say anything but watched as his eyes had bored into me and then changed as he became more and more mortified. We stopped talking after that, and then she moved last year."

Riley leaned forward. "More like avoided each other since, at least until now."

"Yeah, thanks for that. Either way, I have to shadow him until I'm off this trial period. What do I do?"

"I don't think you can do anything," Randy said.

I slouched. "Well, that isn't helpful."

Shelby shook her head. "I don't know, Sophie. I think I'm with Randy. I don't think you can come back from that."

My eyes widened. "Really? I thought you'd be able to think of something, with all your apologies you've had to make."

Shelby crossed her arms. "Yeah, yeah. We get it. I've made lots of mistakes. But honestly, I don't know how you'd make it up to a guy you fully and completely embarrassed. He had feelings for you and tried to make a move, and you not only rejected him, but mortified him. What if that had been you?"

"Ugh, if you can't think of something, then I really screwed up."

Shelby ate another bite of her lunch. "Pretty much. How did he seem last night?"

"He wasn't thrilled. I think I shocked him that I was the new employee and then that he had to be my boss. He also said it was a bad idea."

"Honestly, I would just do your job and give him as little of a headache as possible. Maybe he'll soften up after a while," Shelby suggested.

"Randy? As a guy, what do you think?"

Randy shook his head. "I don't know, but Shelby's idea isn't bad. Maybe if you guys can end up as friends again, it won't be so awkward."

Riley wiggled her eyebrows. "Or maybe kiss him?"

I gasped. "What? Are you out of your mind?"

Shelby giggled. "Is there more to this story that I'm missing?"

I glared at Riley. "No. She's just in denial about Drew."

Shelby scrunched her nose. "What do you mean?"

I sighed. "Remember in the fall when she saw you at the movies to that horror film?"

Shelby nodded. "Of course, I do. I spent the movie trying to figure out what had just happened and how I had gotten there. No one had told me off like that before."

"Eesh, right, well, that same night we saw Drew take our tickets—"

"And I think Sophie has feelings," Riley said.

I rolled my eyes. "I do not; I just don't like the tension."

Shelby's eyebrow rose. "It would be a cool idea. Then all of us could have a guy in our lives."

Riley clapped vigorously. "Yes! That's a perfect plan. Let's get them together instead of just friends."

"Or maybe, you all should listen to the words coming out of my mouth. I just don't want it to be awkward anymore. I don't want a boyfriend or anything crazy. I just hate the guilt I feel when I'm around him, and now I'm forced to be in his presence more than I'd like."

"Time will tell, Sophie. Until then, just don't make anything worse," Randy said.

I could do that, couldn't I? There was no way I liked him. I just wanted things to not feel so awkward anymore.

~

I inhaled deeply as I walked through the theater doors. The rest of the week had gone by too quickly. I wasn't ready to come face to face with Drew again. In school, it was easy not to run into him, but at the theater … well, I wasn't sure I was ready.

I searched the theater lobby for Mr. Martin or Drew. I wasn't sure if Mr. Martin wanted me to check in with him during every shift, but I figured either one would work.

Drew was the first person I saw. This time, instead of by

the ticket podium, he was behind the counter, helping someone with their popcorn and candy. Would I have to do the snack counter too today? Or would they keep me at the ticket podium?

I strolled toward Drew and stopped a few feet away.

Drew checked his watch then met my gaze. "On time. Let's get your headset, and I'll explain what you're doing today."

I nodded and followed Drew to the staff room close to Mr. Martin's room. If it was possible, it was even tinier than his office. A shelf with three cubbies in each row stood against the wall. A small table, chairs, a refrigerator, and a small sink were all that furnished the room.

"If you have any personal items you need to store, there will be a cubby for you. While you are on trial, if you need to store something, just let me know. We have one no one uses just in case." He handed me my headset. "Go ahead put this on. You'll learn a new position today. We'll be behind the snack counter with Courtney."

"Courtney?" The name seemed familiar, but I struggled trying to think of how.

"She's our age, but she doesn't live in Honey Cove. She actually lives not far from the theater."

That's why it was familiar. It was the name Drew had dropped on my first shift. "Okay. Well, you're the leader. I'm here to do whatever."

He strolled from the staffroom to the front lobby.

I hoped I liked Courtney. It might even cut all the guilty tension between us, which I would gladly welcome.

As I approached the snack counter once again, I noticed the petite blonde behind the counter. I watched as she spoke to a customer and handed them their treats. She seemed bubbly and outspoken; maybe we wouldn't hit it off. I wasn't someone who was cheery for no reason. In fact,

I felt the happiest during track. Considering this was nowhere close to track, we might have very little in common.

Drew stood between us both as I passed behind the counter. "Courtney, this is Sophie. Sophie, this is Courtney. Courtney has been here about as long as I have. If you need anything, she's a good person to ask. Courtney, Sophie is our trial employee. She's shadowing me for now. Can you show her the popcorn machine? I'll be back in a bit. Mr. Martin needs me to do a few things."

"No problem," Courtney said. She eyed me as I stood waiting for her to give me directions.

I proffered my hand. "Nice to meet you."

Courtney nodded but didn't shake my hand. "New meat, huh? Always fun. Watch out for Drew though; he likes to play pranks."

My eyes widened. "Drew? No way."

Courtney giggled. "Oh yeah. He's good at it too. He swapped the butter and cheese on an employee once. They poured nacho cheese all over someone's popcorn. They had to redo the whole thing."

"I don't believe you. Drew doesn't do stuff like that at all. He's so serious."

Courtney's eyebrow arched. "Not this Drew. You say that like you know each other."

"Yes. Well, sort of. He lives in my neighborhood. We go to the same school and used to hang out, but I've never seen Drew be like that. Ever."

Courtney shrugged. "Maybe you don't know him like you think you do."

Was that possible? Had he changed since that barbecue? Had we ever really known who he was? I found it hard to believe that someone he worked with knew things about him I had never seen, but why would she lie? She had no reason not to tell the truth, but a prankster was the furthest characteristic from who I knew.

Courtney shifted her stance. "Anyway, let me show you the popcorn machine. The busy hours will hit soon, and you do *not* want to spend that time trying to figure it out."

I followed behind Courtney, seeing over the top of her head as I walked.

"This machine can be temperamental when it wants to be, so make sure you focus on what I say. I'll be in the snack counter with you, but we don't want to fall behind when the customers rush before the movie."

I nodded.

"It's not too many steps to remember. We keep a good bit in the bottom and have the warmer on. If you get below that red line on the side of the glass, you'll need to make more, since it takes a few minutes to pop. We have the bags of kernels that already contain butter below the counter. When it's time to pop more, you focus on the kettle. Lift the kettle lid and dump the contents of the bag into the kettle. Drop the lid then hit the kettle's on button. It will make it on its own. When the popping slows, you shut off the kettle then turn the kettle so it empties into the rest of the popcorn machine, and voila, popcorn! Make sense?"

"I-I think so."

"I can show you now how to make more so you can go through it at least once. If you have questions as you go, let me know. I'll try and get down here. We also have the extra butter in these bottles you squirt onto the popcorn, as well as any other toppings a customer wants."

"That part I know. I've gotten popcorn here before. This is the only theater close enough to my town."

"Are you ready? I'll walk you through a process, and then we'll see how you do."

I nodded and grabbed the bag of kernels and butter.

Courtney watched silently, unless I paused, which only ended up being at the end when she reminded me to empty the kernels into the rest of the machine. "Not bad, Sophie." She surveyed the crowd in the lobby and checked the wall clock behind us. "In about ten minutes, the next wave of people will come through, eager to go into their theater. You ready for that?"

"I think so. If not, I'll ask."

"Sounds good. I'll be down at the other end, but ask over the headset, and I'll hear you like you were next to me."

I nodded and watched as she sauntered to the other end of the counter.

Just like clockwork, the crowd bombarded the counter at exactly the time she said it would. The first few groups ignored the popcorn and went to the candy and self-serve soda sections. Then I got slammed. Four groups in a row wanted two large popcorns each, which left me well below that red line. I utilized the brief pause in my queue to load another batch of popcorn. I remembered the steps and successfully started the batch. At least I could do this correctly.

"Very nice," Drew said.

I startled, nearly knocking over a bottle with butter. "You can't do that! You scared me half to death."

"I'm sorry. I thought you heard me coming. You did that correctly though, so I wanted to tell you. Have you done a few?"

I shook my head. "That was the first one I did alone."

Drew stroked his chin. "Your first? That's impressive. I was watching how you handled your crowd. That was well done too. Efficient, and you made sure to greet each group as you scooped."

I blushed. It was strange to receive a compliment from

Drew. Sure, he was my boss at this point, but it was nice. "Thanks."

He nodded. "I'm back to join you and Courtney, so if you run out of something or need anything, let me know. I'll float between your two ends."

"Sounds good to me. Thanks."

He turned, and I watched as he approached her. He smiled, and his shoulders relaxed.

Courtney smirked and said something, making them both laugh—not a small laugh either but a hearty, inside joke kind of laugh.

He relaxed away from me. Was Courtney right? Was it possible that I really had no idea who Drew was? I shook my head. Did it matter? He would never forgive me anyway.

CHAPTER 7

The birds chirped, and the sun shone upon us as we ran. Riley had texted at the end of my shift to see how it had gone and to plan a morning run. It was the best idea to burn off the unbearable energy I had from being around Drew.

"You better focus if you expect to catch up with me!" Riley shouted from twenty or so feet ahead.

"You wish. I'm thinking and enjoying the weather. It's starting to consistently be warmer, and I am here for it."

"The weather is perfect, but to run, you actually have to move at a pace faster than a walk."

I stuck out my tongue. "Whatever. Let's go then. You're the one whose pace is slower. I'm just not trying to show you up too much."

Riley stopped to jog in place and put her hands out from her hips. "So much trash talk for no audience. You want to race, then let's race." Without warning, she bounded from her spot.

It took a moment for me to register that she had just ran away and then to actually get my feet moving. By the time I had kicked it up to high gear, Riley was a fair distance away. How did she do that? She was the only person I ever knew who barely had to warm up and could launch from her place as fast as possible. She'd had no official training when she moved to Honey Cove, and yet, she performed at the top every time. It was madness, but on most days, I enjoyed the challenge. It kept me focused, sharp—all qualities that helped to push me further in my track stamina and abilities. I only hoped it improved my times when we hit the fall again.

Ahead, Riley had stopped next to Shelby's BMW.

I ran as hard as I could until I reached the door then caught my breath.

"You need a ride?" Shelby asked.

Riley looked at me then at Shelby. "We were doing a run, but I don't know, Sophie, what do you want to do?"

I checked my phone to see how far and long we had been walking and running. "Sure, but what are you doing out anyway?" I said, satisfied with the three miles we had already completed.

"I was actually headed to Riley's house. Needed to get out of the house. The closer we get to the spring festival, the more fidgety my mother becomes, always checking in, and Father isn't much better. They keep hovering."

"Ugh, I hate when my mama hovers. It's the worst, not to mention their timing is always the absolute worst. I have no idea how they manage to time it so well."

"You sure you ran enough, Sophie? You seemed itching to burn off some steam," Riley said.

"I'm sure. Three miles helped, and, as long as I'm not home dealing with my mama or at work with Drew, I'll take it as win."

Riley chuckled.

"Well, get in," Shelby said as she unlocked the doors.

Riley sat up front, while I hopped in the back seat behind

Shelby. It still blew my mind that the three of us hung out. Sure, I was closer to Riley, but Shelby had held true to her word, so why not? I had never expected to be friends with Shelby Rowe, but she was turning out to be a friend I was glad I had.

"So, what's the plan for today?" Riley asked.

"Anything as long as I don't go home yet," I said.

"We could go shopping?" Shelby suggested.

"Nah. I don't feel like shopping," Riley said.

"Agreed."

Shelby tapped her finger on the steering wheel. "Well, I'm game for whatever. Like Sophie said, if I don't have to go home, I'm good with sitting on a couch, watching TV."

Riley giggled. "You two are crazy, but we can hang out at my mom-mom's house. I have new nail polish, or we could see what new movies are streaming."

"Works for me," I said.

Shelby nodded.

We arrived at Riley's fifteen minutes later, unloaded and sat on the porch stairs. Riley and I both stretched to keep our muscles from being sore from our run. It was an important step, one I had learned the hard way several times by skipping.

Shelby shoved her keys and phone into her clutch. "So, Sophie, why'd you need to burn off all this energy?"

I sighed. "Another shift last night with Drew. I feel so guilty around him. Plus, I learned that he is actually a prankster and laid back. I watched him with Courtney, and he never acted like that around me."

"Have you thought about apologizing?" Riley asked.

"Thought about it, yes. Done anything about it, no. What do I say? 'Hey, Drew. So, I'm sorry I made you kiss a dog and then totally ghosted you for five years.' Yeah, no thanks. Not to mention I don't know that I want to bring it up at work.

It's the elephant in the room as it is, but what if it got worse? I couldn't take that."

Shelby moved to the porch swing and sat. "What if it got better?"

"How could it get better?"

"When I had done something to someone, the worst feeling was not knowing how they would take it. I agonized over what they thought and what I should do. I always felt better when I apologized and moved past the original instance, whether or not they agreed. Sometimes the energy is worse because no one is touching it."

"Maybe. I still don't know if I could bear making it worse. He's my boss until this trial is over. Shouldn't I wait?"

Riley crossed her arms. "I think waiting will make it worse. You can say something to him now, see how he reacts, and go from there. Otherwise, you're just torturing yourself. From what you've said, he wants to act professionally, so wait until a shift is over and just bite the bullet. What do you have to lose?"

I scoffed. "Tons. He could get me fired. He could hate me. He—"

"Take it from someone who knows. He could feel however he feels, but that won't change because you apologize. He already feels how he feels about it. The apologizing would help you. If you apologize and he doesn't accept it, you did what you had to and can move on. Any other scenario and you still haven't done something to assuage your guilt."

I harrumphed. "Why are we discussing my issues with Drew? Why should I care what happened? It's an unfortunate turn of events, but Jenna did all the dirty work."

Riley stared at me and shook her head. "Sophie, you know you feel bad because you hurt him. You were friends.

Even if you say you don't *like*, like him, you shared experiences. You care about him on some level."

"Maybe."

Shelby giggled. "I, for one, would love to hear more about this friendship. I mean, were you close enough to really be this upset about being around him?"

"I mean, yeah. The three of us spent a lot of time together. Drew and Jenna used to spend time in our back yard, stargazing with my dad and me. My dad would point out the constellations, and we would squint until we thought we saw it. When he would leave us alone, we made up our own constellations. We were young, but we shared a lot together."

"Do you miss being friends with him?" Riley asked.

I shrugged. "I don't know. Things were so different after my dad died anyway. I don't know how things would have changed."

Shelby squinted against the sun. "What I still don't understand is, why if the three of you were so close, Jenna made the dare in the first place?"

I shrugged. "I wonder that too sometimes. She was devilish on occasion, but she generally had her reasons."

"You never thought to ask her why?"

"Me? No! I wanted to forget the whole thing happened afterwards. Talking to her about it would have made me remember and relive it over and over even more than I did."

Riley and Shelby exchanged glances.

"What?" I asked.

"Nothing …" Shelby paused. "It's just, what if the knowledge of his feelings for you changed the dynamic in her head? I mean, what if *she* liked Drew?"

Jenna liked Drew? I had never thought about that, but even as I considered it, I stifled giggles. "I don't know, but I doubt it."

Shelby shrugged. "It just seems odd. Cruelty comes from

a special place, and it's not generally directed to people we care about. Just seems like something shifted."

"Well, regardless, the damage is done and I have no plan to deal with it. I'd say it's been five years; why does it matter? Only if I feel this guilty still, I can't imagine what he feels."

Riley walked closer and nudged my shoulder. "Let's go in. You can take a shower and borrow some clothes."

"A shower sounds nice. I can smell myself, which I don't enjoy."

We followed Riley into the house. I listened for sounds of her mom or mom-mom as we ascended the stairs. I hadn't paid attention if their vehicles were in the driveway, but it was fairly quiet for the house if they were. "Where is everyone?"

Riley turned briefly as she climbed the stairs. "Mom is at work at the post office, and Mom-Mom is probably at her gardening meetings. You know how she is about her flowers."

I shrugged and followed Riley as she gathered towels and clothes for me. "Thanks."

She nodded.

I entered the bathroom as Shelby and Riley walked to her room. I contemplated what they had said as I prepared the shower. Were they right? Should I just apologize, even if it did nothing but make me feel better? It couldn't be that easy. We had avoided each other at school; it had to be a deep-rooted embarrassment for Drew or he would have let it go.

And what about Shelby's theory of Jenna liking Drew? I couldn't imagine that had been her motive. She had been uninterested in guys at the time, or at least she used to say she was. I stepped into the hot water and let it pour over me, releasing the tension from their comments and last night's shift.

I needed to refocus. I had plenty other things to deal with, like Mama's new boyfriend. Instead of worrying about Drew, I should be convincing Mama she needed to let Rowan go. Dad deserved more time. He deserved to be remembered, not to be replaced, and it was my job to remind them.

~

"Does this movie work?" Riley asked.

Shelby and I nodded.

"Okay. So, do you want to paint your nails, or are you two good?"

"I'll check out what you have," I said.

"Sure. I haven't gone to the nail salon in a few weeks. It's time for a refresh."

Riley giggled then disappeared to grab her nail polishes. She returned with a tub of different colored polishes.

I searched for a purple and found a light purple at the bottom of the tub.

Shelby perused the colors until she settled on a light pink, while Riley grabbed bright turquoise.

"So how are things for you, Shelby?" I asked.

She shrugged. "It's fine, minus the hovering from my parents. I'll be happy when the spring festival is over. Only two more weeks and it'll be in full swing. We start the scavenger hunts and punch cards next week. So many moving parts."

"Based on what Randy told me, you both have it covered though," Riley said.

Shelby unscrewed the nail polish and focused on her nails. "We do, but it's a lot of pressure. I have a feeling that if I nail this spring festival, I can finally be off probation with my parents."

"That'd be nice," I said.

"Yeah, it would. I'm not that worried about it. My mother

hasn't said much about my friends at this point, but I still worry she'll backpedal. She was so mad in January when I went over her head to my father."

Riley cringed. "Yeah, let's hope that doesn't happen. I don't want to see my name on the Buzz app ever again. I'm honestly surprised she didn't retaliate from you going to him."

Shelby shook her head. "Mother isn't stupid. Father is the head of the house. If there's anything she believes, it's that the patriarch gets the final word."

I chuckled. "That sounds barbaric." I shifted toward Riley. "What if your name appears because of track?"

Riley tapped her finger to her chin. "Maybe, but nothing about my family or Randy or anything like that."

"Amen to that," I said.

"How about the other elephant in your life?" Riley asked.

Shelby's eyebrows knitted. "The, what?"

I nudged Riley's elbow. "She means Luke. She just isn't very good with humor."

Riley stuck out her tongue. "Hush you, but yes, things with Luke. How's it going?"

Shelby didn't look up from her nails. "It's not."

Riley's eyes widened. "Why not?"

Shelby sighed. "How is it supposed to go anywhere if he's at boarding school? He might be home for Easter, but he isn't so sure anymore. I don't even know if anything is there."

"Do you want it to be there?" I asked and grabbed a Q-tip to fix the edges of my nails.

"I have no idea. I honestly hated him before, then I realized I was judging him the same way I complained about other people judging me. He really helped me over break before he left, but now school and the council stuff is getting so hectic, plus his schedule, and we barely talk anymore."

Riley frowned. "Well, change it. Maybe you could go

there for a weekend if he can't come here? Or maybe you meet him for dinner there?"

"I don't know if my mother would let me drive there during school."

I held my hand in front and waved it for the polish to dry. "Well, you won't know if you don't ask."

"Love advice from the person who refuses love exists?" Shelby asked.

I harrumphed. "Love is fine for other people, just not me."

"Or your mama," Riley added.

I glared. "Don't go there."

She raised her hands in defense. "I'm just saying. Would it be so bad if your mama moved on and found someone who made her happy?"

"Yes, it would, and I don't want to discuss it."

"Fair enough."

Shelby arched her eyebrow. "What about you, Riley? How are things with you and Randy. You two are adorable, but are you still not *dating*?"

Riley tilted her head. "Dating is a strong word. We are just taking our time."

Shelby looked unimpressed. "You've been taking your time for a while. Don't you want to date him?"

"Well, of course, I'd date him."

"So, it's Randy that's stopping it?"

I leaned back and waited for her answer. This should be interesting, and I had to say I was curious to see what she thought about the situation.

"No, not really." Riley sighed. "I don't know either. I like him … a lot. We mesh so well and are a great partnership, but, if he isn't ready, I don't want to push him."

Shelby shifted the pillow behind her back. "Have you asked him about it?"

"No. I don't want to bother him about it."

I felt bad for Riley. I knew she didn't need the title, but it would be uncomfortable for anyone at some point. The question was, where was her line?

I glanced at all our hands, painted to perfection—well, as close to perfection as an unprofessional could manage. The conversation quieted as we settled in and watched the movie Riley had chosen. It was a comedy and was perfect to offset the heavy mood in the room. If only I could offset the heavy mood in my life, things would be good.

CHAPTER 8

My comfy bed didn't curb the incessant tossing and turning I seemed to be doing nonstop. It was Sunday morning already, and what was worse was I had to attend a family brunch—with Rowan. I peeped from under the covers to check the time—8 a.m. I didn't have much longer to waste before I needed to get ready, and avoiding the brunch was impossible. Mama wouldn't allow it.

I kicked the covers from my bed, chose an outfit from my messy closet and trudged to the bathroom. If I didn't want to be there, then maybe looking the part would placate Mama.

My facewash burst over my skin, waking me up ever so slightly. I knew Mama wanted this brunch to go better than the surprise visit before, but I wasn't ready, and I didn't understand why she couldn't accept that. Not to mention I had a shift at the theater today. I just wanted to relax, do a little of my schoolwork and go to work. Brunches were nowhere on the itinerary.

My shirt was a tad wrinkly; at least the material didn't make the wrinkles look sloppy but more a part of the design.

I searched for my slip-ons and walked to the kitchen. Surprisingly, I was the only one in the front of the house. Everyone else must have been getting ready.

The refrigerator was stocked with sports drinks, waters, and juices. Mama always kept the house stocked lately, and I now wondered how much of that had to do with Rowan and less with us. I grabbed a water and sat at the kitchen table.

Mama strolled around the corner as she hummed softly. "Glad to see you're already dressed. Working on Caleb and, in about twenty minutes, Rowan should be here."

I smiled, because if I had opened my mouth, things that would irritate her and would get me in trouble would spew out, and well, I didn't need to start this early.

Caleb sauntered into the kitchen as he attempted to tuck in his shirt.

My face scrunched. "Why are you tucking in a T-shirt? That looks ridiculous."

Caleb frowned. "Aren't you supposed to tuck in your shirt?"

Mama giggled. "A collared shirt, yes. T-shirts, no."

"Well, what do I do now?"

Mama guided Caleb into the hallway and to what I assumed was his room.

I shook my head. Caleb was a mess. He had no idea what style was. Thankfully, Mama agreed and stopped him before he looked ridiculous and it rubbed off on me.

My hands fidgeted with the hem of my shirt. I couldn't stop moving. It was like if I somehow stopped, I'd have to deal with the situation in front of me. I didn't want Rowan to arrive. I didn't want to go to brunch as a *family* with some strange substitute for my dad. This man couldn't replace him, and I didn't understand why everyone else acted like he could.

A knock sounded from the front door, and my stomach slammed into my feet.

"Be right there!" Mama called out.

I sighed and tiptoed to the front window. I pulled back the cream-colored curtain ever so slightly and stared at the man trying to invade my family.

Rowan wore khakis, a polo shirt, and a navy-colored blazer. He looked like a cross between a golfer and a frat boy, neither of which my dad would have ever been described as.

I clenched my fist and had to actively force it to open back up.

Mama was moving on, and she was doing it with someone so different from Dad it was like she was *purposely* erasing who he was from this house.

Mama wiped her hands on her jeans and walked to the door. She eyed me warily then opened the door. Her smile spread as she beheld Rowan.

Caleb reentered the family room, and I watched his expression nearly matching Mama's as he noticed Rowan.

"Good morning," Rowan said.

"Hey, Rowan. Awesome blazer," Caleb said.

They both fist bumped, and I did my best to not vomit in my mouth.

Great, everyone is in love with this preppy man but me.

Mama stared between Caleb and me. "Ready to head out?" Mama held open the door as we filtered through.

I hovered by the sidewalk, waiting for some indication of what vehicle we would take. I didn't know if Mama would drive or if Rowan would, but either way, I was less than thrilled to be piled into the same vehicle with him.

Mama locked the door and strolled toward Rowan's Porsche SUV.

Caleb and I hopped into the back seats. At least there would be some separation. I buckled my seatbelt and surveyed the area. Rowan's back seats were super clean, so he either just detailed them himself or rarely had anyone back here. It was devoid of any other clues about him.

Caleb leaned over to me and whispered, "Do you think Rowan will be around for Easter?"

"I don't know. Do I look like a fortune teller?"

"What's wrong with you?"

"Nothing, but why ask stupid questions?"

Caleb slumped in his seat and turned away.

Over Easy's loomed ahead as Rowan parked. I sighed inwardly; this was not what I wanted to do whatsoever. My phone buzzed with Riley's message: *How's brunch?*

She had quite good timing.

I replied quickly, *I'll let you know if I survive it.* I shoved the phone into my pocket and got out. The day was warm, the sky blue. It would be perfect for a run. I sighed as I followed everyone else to a booth.

Over Easy's was the local diner with an uncanny expression of its theme to be absolutely everywhere. The décor didn't just have subtle hints of eggs but an obverse and in-your-face type of presence. It may be over the top, but it felt like home. Honey Cove would be amiss without Over Easy's, and I would be amiss without their food. The only highlight of this annoying brunch was that I could eat at Over Easy's.

Betty, the staple waitress, sat us in the corner booth at the far left.

Mama sat across from me, while Rowan sat across from Caleb. It was a poor choice to have Caleb and I next to each other, but at least no one sat me next to Rowan.

Betty smiled as she steadied her pen against the notepad. "What can I get y'all?"

Mama spoke first. "We'll start with drinks and then will

need a few minutes to decide on food. I'll take a sweet tea with lemon."

"Dr. Pepper," Caleb said.

"Water, no lemon," I said.

Rowan stayed silent for a few seconds. "Coffee, black and a small water with lemon."

"Coming right up," Betty said and walked away.

Mama looked around the table at us while I tried to hide behind my menu, avoiding her gaze. "This is certainly nice, don't y'all think?"

"I'm so hungry," Caleb said.

I rolled my eyes. "You're always hungry."

Rowan chuckled. "I remember when I was your age. I ate all the time, but nowhere near the amount I ate when I was a junior in high school."

"Oh boy. There will be nothing left," Mama said.

Caleb grinned. "That's right. Watch out, I'm gonna get bigger."

"A bigger head," I muttered.

Caleb glared at me but stayed silent.

I studied my menu like it was a treasure map. The longer I looked, the less time I'd have to engage in a conversation with anyone—which, if I was being honest, was perfectly fine with me. Pretending we were a family was ridiculous, and I didn't know how, but I would ensure to convince my mama.

"Everyone knows what they want?" Mama asked.

We all nodded and stayed silent as we waited for Betty.

Betty strolled to our table while balancing the drinks we had ordered. After passing them out, she paused at the end of the table, her pen and notebook ready. "Are we all set?"

Mama looked at each of us and nodded. "I'll take your peach French toast, eggs over easy, and sausage patties."

Caleb closed his menu. "I'll take your five-high stack of pancakes, hash browns, and bacon."

Rowan smiled at Betty. "I'll have the peach French toast, eggs over easy, and sausage patties as well."

They ordered the same meal? How cutesy of them.

"I'll have the strawberry-cream waffles with bacon, no eggs."

Betty nodded and collected the menus then walked away to enter our orders.

Mama tapped the end of her straw on the table until the plain straw popped up. After a long sip of her sweet tea, she eyed me warily. "So, Sophie, you have work today, right?"

I nodded, focusing solely on my drink in front of me.

"I was wondering if Rowan could drive you?"

My gaze snapped up and stared between Mama and Rowan. Mama's face implored me to respond appropriately, while Rowan looked gleeful and open to doing whatever Mama asked. I was trapped, and she knew it.

"Sure, but where will you be?"

"I must go into work this afternoon, and Rowan was free."

"Oh, okay. Yeah, fine."

It was anything but fine. I wanted to scream, shout, and kick my way out of this deal, but, if I did, Mama would become even more insufferable, and that was good for no one.

"Caleb, do you have all your homework done for tomorrow?" Mama asked.

"Mostly."

Mama eyed Caleb warily. "Mostly? That's not a yes. What's left?"

"I have a history paper to write."

"A paper? When is it due?"

"Tomorrow."

Mama's eyes widened. "Please tell me you've started it."

"Well…"

"Caleb Joseph!"

I smirked behind my drink. He was so going to get it now.

"You waited until the last minute to start this paper? How long have you had the assignment?"

"Possibly two weeks."

Mama's head rested into her hands as she looked at her feet. "Caleb, how will you manage this paper when I need to work today? You must keep your grades up. Just because you're about to graduate middle school, doesn't mean you can slack off."

Caleb raised his hands and shrugged. "I'll figure something out. I always do."

Mama shook her head and stared at Caleb as if she wanted to obliterate him with her eyes.

"I could help," Rowan said.

Of course, he would offer. Who did he think he was—a knight in shining armor? This was absurd. Besides, no one ever helped me on my assignments; the little dweeb could deal with the mess he made.

Caleb panned between Mama and Rowan. "Mama, is that okay?"

Mama nibbled on the corner of her lip. "I suppose, but, Caleb, I swear, if you do this again, you are so grounded for the rest of the school year."

"Deal."

Rowan smiled and sipped his coffee.

The three of them chitchatted as I sat in silence, avoiding eye contact and desperately wishing I could text anyone at this point to avoid this brunch. When the food finally arrived, I ensured every bite I took was calculated just perfectly that I wouldn't have to contribute to the conversation. Luckily, no one called me out on it. Unfortunately, I wouldn't be so lucky when I had to ride with Rowan to work.

~

*M*ama pulled me aside before I strolled through the front door. "Please be on your best behavior. Rowan is doing me a favor by driving you to the theater. Make sure to use your manners. Okay?"

I nodded.

"You promise?"

I uncrossed my arms. "Okay, yeah. Fine."

Mama squinted at me, almost began speaking, then stopped and nodded.

I took that as my cue to run away, even though I didn't want to get to my destination. I tapped my pants pockets to ensure I had brought everything I needed for work.

Rowan smiled and tapped his hands on his steering wheel to an inaudible beat as I walked around to the passenger door.

I inhaled deeply as I gripped the handle. After a count of three, I hopped into the front seat.

The radio blared some pop station as Rowan bobbed his head.

I sighed. This was going to feel like the longest car ride of my existence.

Rowan let a few songs pass in silence then turned down the radio's volume. "I know I'm not who you want to drive you to the theater, but I'm glad you agreed." He looked at me then back on the road. "I thought we could take this chance to get to know each other. You don't know me. I don't really know you. What do you think?"

I shrugged because what I wanted to say wasn't appropriate. I wasn't allowed to tell him I didn't care who he was, because he wouldn't be around long enough for me to need the information. I couldn't tell him I didn't care, because he wasn't my father and would never replace him. I couldn't tell him I didn't care, because he didn't earn the right to know me yet.

"Awesome. So, you know where I work and that I like to play golf, but I'm one of four siblings. I'm actually in the middle of three sisters. We're all pretty close, but no one lives nearby."

I lost track of what Rowan said by the time he went into his sisters' names. I wasn't dating him. I didn't want him around; why did he think an information dump of his life would win me over? Less was more, and he obviously never got that memo.

Rowan cleared his throat. "What about you?"

I shrugged.

"Any interesting facts about yourself I should know?"

"Not really. Just a typical high schooler."

Rowan chuckled. "Not according to your mother."

I turned slightly. "Oh?"

Rowan's grin widened. "Oh yeah. She's so proud of you in track and in school. She says she only worries about how you're feeling."

My eyebrow arched. "Why?"

Rowan shrugged. "She doesn't go too much into that, but I suspect she's just being a mama bear worried about her cub."

I crossed my arms.

"That's not a bad thing. All moms worry about their kids."

"Mm-hmm."

Rowan glanced at me.

I turned my body away, hoping he'd realize the conversation was over. Mama had no right to discuss me with him, especially her fears about me. And why would she be worried about how I felt? Caleb was the loose cannon. I never waited on my school assignments. I always did what I agreed to accomplish. Why would there be anything *worrying* about me?

Thankfully, Rowan ran out of time to push it. The theater loomed just in front of us. He pulled next to the curb by the front door.

I opened the door as he called my name.

"Sophie. Thanks for letting me get a chance to get to know you. I know you don't have to do that. I appreciate it and just wanted you to know."

I nodded, shoved the door closed then walked to the front of the theater without looking back. The whole situation irked me. Mama and her pushiness, Caleb and his obvious acceptance, and Rowan with his never-ending endearing personality was too much.

The bustling crowds and the intense volume bombarded me as I entered the theater. It was by far more crowded than I had expected it to be on a Sunday afternoon. I peered over the crowd, looking for the familiar face I needed to shadow. I had no idea where he would be since, so far, I always found him in a different spot on my shifts. Based on the way my day had gone already, I fully expected him to be working in a new location—adding one more thing for me to learn.

Surprisingly, Drew stood next to Courtney by the concessions. His hair peeked through the bottom of his hat and over the tops of his ears. He looked relaxed as his shoulders shook from his laughing.

I slowly approached them, not wanting to interrupt.

Courtney saw me first and smiled. "Hey, Soph. That's okay, right? I just feel like I *have* to call you Soph."

"I don't care."

"Cool." Courtney turned her wrist and checked the time. "Welp, break time's over. See ya later, Drew." She winked at me as she sauntered away.

I teetered back and forth, waiting for Drew to

acknowledge me. By the time he turned, my expression had soured. Today was only getting worse by the second.

Drew gazed at me then focused on the notebook at his side.

I cleared my throat, waiting for him to let me know where I needed to go for my shift. When it had finally felt too long to continue to be ignored, I spoke up. "Hello? Anyone in there?"

Drew's brows knitted. "Yeah. I can see you. Just relax. I need to figure out where you'll be the most useful tonight."

"The most useful? That doesn't sound encouraging."

"It's the best business move. As you can see, we are swamped today."

"Exactly, so shouldn't this decision be made quickly."

Drew stopped leaning against the counter and crossed his arms. "Excuse me?"

I mimicked his stance. "Well, if we are so busy, shouldn't I be put to work sooner rather than later?"

"You will be momentarily. Or *would have* been if you didn't interrupt me." He shook his head. He teetered between watching me and staring at his notebook. The repeated action drove spikes farther into my nerves. "Go check people's tickets tonight. Put on your headset and check in thirty minutes from now."

"Thirty minutes? Why?"

Drew's gaze narrowed. "Because I asked you to." Drew dropped the notebook on the counter and adjusted his hat. "This is why I didn't want to be responsible for you. Typical Sophie, always worried about herself. You wouldn't have taken that attitude with Mr. Martin. It has been three shifts, and you're already abusing the fact that we know each other from before."

"I—"

"Save it, Sophie. I'm not interested in your excuses. I gave you a direction, get going."

I had never been rendered speechless by someone else so swiftly. I might have been a little impatient but was I really so worried about myself to the point that someone like Drew had noticed? Not to mention, did this mean he was done working with me? That was not a scenario I wanted enacted. I needed this job to avoid my house and Rowan. If Drew gave up on me, I was sunk.

I shuffled my feet toward the staff lounge. I only had a few hours to devise a plan to fix this. But, whatever I did, it had to be successful.

<h1 style="text-align:center">CHAPTER 9</h1>

I kicked the pebbles on the sidewalk as I waited. The rest of my shift hadn't gotten better. Drew avoided me the rest of the night, except for the check-ins. This was my last chance to get him to listen to me and believe that I truly was sorry.

The breeze had picked up since this afternoon and swished my pants by my ankles. Every time the door opened, my heart jumped, until I realized it was just another family leaving after viewing a movie.

Finally, Drew exited the theater.

I knew the second he noticed me.

His body tensed, and the skin around his eyes went taut. He certainly wasn't excited to see me, but how could I blame him?

I stepped toward him. "Can we talk?"

"Sophie," Drew said with a sigh. "I must get home."

I reached out my hand and pulled it back. "I know, but I wanted to ask if you could drive me home."

"What? Why?"

"No one can pick me up for another two hours. You'd be

doing me a favor. Please? I know I'm not your favorite person, but we don't live that far from each other. You can just drive to your house, and I'll walk from there."

He fiddled with the keys in his pocket, creating the unmistakable clanking sound. "There's absolutely no one else who could drive you? Riley? No one?"

I shook my head.

"Fine."

I resisted jumping to celebrate my success. The first part of the plan had worked; now I just had to apologize and get him to believe me, and I was set.

Drew strode toward his car, not looking back to see if I was keeping up. He unlocked his car door and used the unlock button on the inside of his door to let me in.

I studied the floorboards of his black compact car. It took me longer than I had expected to gain the courage I needed to actually talk to Drew one on one. In all the scheming, I had forgotten how little we really talked when I wasn't working as his employee.

"This is a nice song. Do you know who the artist is?" I asked, cringing at how horrible of a transition this was.

Drew tilted his head, but his gaze remained on the road.

I leaned closer to the radio, as if that was where the speakers were. "Is it new? I honestly can't tell."

Drew sighed. "No. It's an older song. The band is Shinedown."

My eyebrow arched. "Shinedown? I didn't realize you listened to them."

He shrugged.

"They're a cool band."

"Sophie, what's this about? We haven't just *talked* in forever. Why tonight?"

My posture slouched. "I know. I'm sorry. Ugh, Drew. I really *am* sorry."

"Okay, but again, why now? We have successfully ignored each other for years. Why now?"

"I know. Truly, I never expected to shadow you at the theater. It was my last hope to get a job, and I totally didn't remember you worked there. I should have, and if you feel like I interrupted your territory, I would completely understand."

He sighed. "Sophie, I'm not some animal peeing on everything to make it my area. I don't have issues with you working at the theater. I wish I wasn't your boss, but I'm not like that. I figured you would at least remember that about me, but maybe not."

"No, you're right. I do know that. I'm totally screwing this up." I bent my head into my hands and rubbed my face.

"Ruining what?"

"This apology and explanation."

Drew chuckled.

"I know you aren't shallow or territorial like that. What I meant was I kind of invaded your life, screwed with our new natural order, then treated you poorly tonight. All of which totally wasn't your fault, and yet, you still end up being the one who's affected by it."

"So, what happened then?"

"It's my family."

He shifted in his seat. "Is your mom okay?"

"Yeah. It's not her. She's ... well, she's dating. Her boyfriend dropped me off at the theater tonight and just tried so hard to get to know me. I may have lost my mind following the experience."

"*May?*"

"Okay, definitely lost my mind. I never wanted to disrespect you in any way. The energy just boiled over from before. I promised Mama I wouldn't embarrass her when he drove me to work, and, in order to keep that promise, I had to suck in everything. I guess when I saw you, it all came out. And you're right. It isn't fair, and it isn't okay. I don't get to use our past at work, and I totally know that, except I crossed the line."

"Well, I can appreciate your apology. But, Sophie, please don't do it again. I'm not trying to make work feel like that for me, and if it does, I can't keep being your boss."

"I completely understand. I wouldn't blame you if you told Mr. Martin I shouldn't continue."

"What? I'm not saying that. You're a hard worker, Sophie. I would merely tell him I think Courtney should train you instead."

"But wouldn't that look poorly to Mr. Martin?"

"No. He trusts me. If I told him you're a hard worker, I just don't think it's a good fit for *me*; he won't take that out on you."

"I don't know how that would be possible and not still impact how Mr. Martin saw me." I shook my head. "I don't want anyone to suffer here. And I promise, I would never cross that line at work again. I swear."

"Okay. We can take it shift by shift."

I smiled. "Thank you."

He nodded and refocused on the road.

I wasn't sure how I'd managed to accomplish that, but it had worked, and for now, that would be enough.

~

The hood felt warm from the engine. I stood by the front of Drew's car, trying to figure out how I could thank him and also apologize for the last time I had hurt him badly, because, quite honestly, I wanted that out of the way too. "Thanks for the ride. You really helped me out."

Drew shoved his hands in his front pockets. "It's the right

thing to do. I couldn't leave you stranded at the theater for two hours. That wouldn't be very safe. Plus, what kind of boss would that make me?"

"A normal one? I'm not really your responsibility. Still, I want you to know I appreciate it. I was hoping we could discuss something else too."

Drew's eyebrow arched. "Like …?"

I fiddled with the edge of my shirt. "The whole Jenna, barbeque thing?"

Drew's eyed widened. "The infamous barbeque." He crossed his arms. "I honestly never thought you would mention that day ever in your life."

"Honestly? That was the plan."

Drew chuckled. "Figures as much. So, why now?"

"I just think that, with everything, it would be better if we cleared the air. I noticed how you are around everyone else at work, and it just feels like I bring you down or something. I don't want to do that. I also never fessed up to my action in the whole thing. I shouldn't have let Jenna do that. It wasn't right."

Drew's face scrunched. "You think the tension is because a dog kissed me? Sophie, it wasn't like I didn't own a dog and have dog kisses before. Not to mention, it has been five years since that happened."

My eyebrows knitted together. "Then what caused the tension?"

"You really don't understand, do you?"

I shook my head.

"We had all been friends, Sophie. We were as close to each other as I'd imagine you, Riley, and all are. After that happened, you and Jenna avoided me little by little until Jenna moved, then you completely and utterly avoided me. So what, I kissed a dog. It was a stupid dare. What sucked was you acted like I had never existed. I had to find new friends, and at neighborhood parties, it was always as if something was missing. *That* is why I went along with the ignoring. I had apparently never mattered to begin with."

My shoulders slumped. He thought the exact opposite of what I had done all that for. "I'm so sorry, Drew. I-I didn't know how to approach you after I knew you'd be willing to kiss me."

"It was a dare, Sophie. You knew how Jenna got when it came to that crap. How was I supposed to get out of it? She would have done far worse if I bailed than if I attempted the dare."

I crossed my arms. "So, you didn't have feelings for me?"

"Sophie, even if I did, what does it honestly matter? We could have gotten over it, but you never wanted to. It hurt me more to lose my friends than to kiss a dog. I was around when your dad died. I was there for you. I hadn't expected to disappear from your life. So, when you successfully avoided me and seemed like it never mattered, I figured I might as well give you your wish."

"Then why do you seem so upset to be around me at work?"

Drew exhaled, ran his hands through his hair and replaced his hat. "There is a lot of damage in our past. You avoid even my gaze in the hallway at school, then at the theater, I *have* to be around you. It's exhausting having to always be aware of where you are when I know you want nothing to do with me."

"Oh, I see." I had no idea he felt that way. I sounded like an awful person in his eyes. I had been worried about his feelings for me, and instead, I should have paid attention to how I ended up treating him. Was I so allergic to someone liking me that I couldn't have put that aside?

Drew drug his shoe against the blacktop. "I should get inside. Are you sure you're okay to walk home?"

"Yeah. I'll be fine. Thanks, Drew." I turned and headed toward the neighborhood drive. How had I been so severely mistaken? Thoughts swirled around as I walked to my house, leaving me unsettled. When I arrived, I opened the front door, shut and locked it and strolled toward my room.

"Sophie? Is that you?" Mama asked.

"Yeah, it's me. I locked the door."

"Okay, thanks. Can you come to my room a minute?"

I walked down the hallway of our ranch home to the first door on the right. Mama's room was in the front of the house, while Caleb had a room in the back, and mine ended up on the side.

Mama sat on her bed, rifling through papers. She paused when I walked through her doorway.

"Yes, Mama?"

"How was work?"

"Fine."

"I was surprised to see you texted me not to come get you. How'd you get home?"

"A friend offered to drive me."

Mama's eyebrows rose. "Okay. I wanted to chat with you about something. Can you have a seat?"

Oh man. I settled on her sage armchair she used to read in the corner of her room.

"I wanted to talk about Rowan."

My stomach sank. Why was everything always about Rowan lately? I needed a break; this was ridiculous.

"I wanted to get your opinion on Rowan. You both sat in the car today, and I was just curious to see what you thought."

I remained silent. However, even though I had expected her to start this conversation, this was clearly not what I had pictured.

"You can tell me anything, Sophie. I want you to remember that."

I clenched my teeth. "He's fine."

Mama's eyebrow rose. "Fine? That's it? You describe people on TV more than that. Seriously, how do you feel?"

"Mama, what do you want me to say?"

"How you feel."

"He's fine as a person, sure. He's fine. Seems motivated and carefree."

"But …?"

"But I don't think you should be dating."

Mama's arms crossed. "And why not?"

"Because of Dad, or have you forgotten about him?"

She exhaled loudly. "Of course, I haven't forgotten about him, Sophie. He was my husband after all, but it was almost six years ago."

"So? We barely speak of him anymore. I can't imagine what you'll do once Rowan barges more into our lives. I don't want him around. I don't want him thinking he can take Dad's place."

"Sophie—"

I left before she finished the sentence, slammed my door and launched onto my bed.

The door creaked.

"Go away, Mama!" I shouted without lifting my head.

"It's not Mama," Caleb said.

I jolted up and stared at my brother. "What do you want?"

"To talk to you."

"About what?"

"How you were with Mama. I can hear her crying in her room."

"What? No, you can't. Why would she be crying?"

Caleb crossed his arms. "For being a big sister, you sure are dense. You upset her."

"Obviously, dweeb, but how could what I said upset her?"

"Maybe because for the first time in a long time, Mama is happy, and you're stepping all over it."

"Well, maybe she should consider how we feel about Dad."

"You mean how *you* feel, right? Because I think Rowan is a great guy. Mama is happy, and you're being selfish. We lost Dad, but she lost her husband. Do you really think she forgot about him?"

"I don't have to talk to you about this. Get out of my room!"

Caleb backed up. "Fine, but think about what you're doing. Mama would do anything for us, and if you think that doesn't mean leave a guy she really cares about, then you're wrong. Do you really want to be the cause for why she's unhappy?" He shook his head and shut my door.

What did he know? He barely remembered Dad. He was only in eighth grade. He should stay in his own lane and worry about school. He didn't know what he was talking about.

*L*unch never sounded so good in my entire life. Food wasn't even my motivation. I had to talk to Riley and Shelby about yesterday. After my conversation with Drew, my sleep was fitful at best and nonexistent at its worst. Eventually, I gave up. They had to know what to do. They just had to.

I darted toward our table.

Shelby and Riley already sat across from each other.

I plopped down next to Shelby.

Their eyes widened.

"You okay?" Riley asked.

"No. Not really."

Shelby looked from me to Riley. "Okay. Do you want to talk about it?"

"It's a long story."

Riley reached across the table and patted my hand. "We're here for you. What happened?"

"Yesterday was rough."

"You had to work yesterday, right? Was it something with Drew?" Riley asked.

I shook my head. "Well, yes, kind of. He was part of it. We actually talked. I had him drive me home."

Riley's eyebrow arched. "Drew took you home? Is that a good thing?" She gasped. "Did something happen?"

"No. We just talked. Get your head out of the gutter."

Shelby chuckled. "She just wishes to live vicariously through you."

"Well, soon enough, she can live my life instead of me if she wants."

Riley's hand stopped halfway to her mouth. "Woah. This really isn't good, is it?"

"No. It started with the brunch. We all went to Over Easy's *like a family*. Mama's words, not mine. Rowan drove with us, and, if that wasn't bad enough, to be stuck at a table without being able to get out of it, Mama couldn't take me to work. Rowan offered, and before I knew it, everything was settled, and he would drive me. Mama made me promise not to be rude again. He talked about himself. I didn't hear half of it. He wanted to *bond* or something stupid. I don't want anything to do with that."

Shelby's face scrunched. "How does that lead to Drew?"

"Well, I may have taken it out on him once I got to work. I was antsy, and it was crowded. He ignored my arrival for what felt like forever, and I had to do something to not feel frustrated with my Mama and Rowan. I snapped."

Riley set her fork on her plate. "You didn't."

I nodded. "I'm not proud of it. That's why I had Drew drive me home. I wanted to apologize. He finally agreed to take it shift by shift as long as it never happened again. He was upset I had used our past to insult him and be snarky. When we got to his house, I remembered what you both had said, and I thought maybe I should apologize about the dare too."

Shelby's eyes widened. "You took our advice?"

"Yes, which turned out well. I think? I mean, at least I found out why things got so awkward. He was more upset about Jenna and me growing apart from him. He said it was like he was nonexistent and had never mattered. He figured that because I had avoided him at school, that's what I wanted. So, he did what I wanted."

"Interesting," Riley said as she tore a piece of bread from her roll.

"I asked what the deal was at work, and again, he basically felt uncomfortable, because he didn't think I wanted anything to do with him. We were both totally wrong about the whole situation."

"So, that sounds positive. Why did the day or night go horribly wrong?"

"Because Mama bombarded me when I walked through the door. She asked me to come to her room to discuss Rowan and what I thought about him, I said he's fine as a human being but she shouldn't be dating." I took a bite of my sandwich. "I also accused her of forgetting my father and that I didn't want to see how much further she pushed his memory from our home with Rowan involved."

Shelby leaned back. "Wow. When you snap, you snap."

"Yeah. And there's more."

"More?" Riley asked.

"I walked out before she could finish, and when I got to my room, Caleb burst in. He basically gave me a lecture for how I treated Mama. He said she was crying and that I needed to think about what I had said to her."

"That's a doozy."

"Tell me about it. He's a dweeb, but I didn't want to make her cry. If that was even true. They just won't listen to me. Don't my feelings matter too?"

Riley nodded. "Absolutely. You need to have a plan

though. Maybe make her think you're trying to connect with Rowan."

I scrunched my nose as if I smelled something gross. "No, thanks. I don't want her to think everything is suddenly fine and dandy. If she thinks things are going well, who knows what steps they'll take next. I don't want more. I want less."

Shelby twisted her ring around and around.

"What?" I asked Shelby. "You look like you have something to say."

"Now hear me out."

I crossed my arms. "Okay."

"What if your brother has a point?"

My jaw slackened. "Excuse me?"

"What if Rowan does make her happy?"

"So what if he does?"

"Well, do you want her to be alone for forever?"

"I don't know." I sighed. "No, but Rowan? He's not it."

Riley tilted her head as her eyes pleaded with me. "Unfortunately, Sophie, your Mama gets to decide who makes her happy."

"And, what? I don't get a say in it?"

"I don't mean it like that. I know what it feels like to have your parents throw you a curveball, but we can't force them to like or want what we want. You don't have to be best friends with him, but if your Mama wants him in her life and he treats her well, is that such a bad thing?"

"I think so." I wiggled farther down in my seat. "This sucks."

"Welcome to getting older," Shelby said.

I tightened my grip around my chair. I didn't like the idea that maybe I had been selfish. My feelings mattered too. I had to fight for them, even if it upset Mama.

"Well, let's not grow up, and instead, let's do something this weekend. Something fun. I need a change of scenery."

Shelby tapped her chin and then winked. "I've got it. There's a party at Brian's house—the football captain—on Friday. Should be a good one."

Riley grimaced. "A party?"

I leaned forward and grinned. "Oh yeah. That's perfect. Riley, you must at least once in your Honey Cove High experience. Come on please?" I puffed out my bottom lip and batted my eyelashes.

"Fine, but hopefully Randy can come too. I guess I'll drive."

"Speaking of, where is he?" I asked.

Riley shrugged. "Said he had to miss lunch today. Something to do with his family. Not sure."

"Everything okay?" Shelby asked.

"I think so. He didn't seem like it was a big deal, just wouldn't be here."

Our conversation shifted away from my issues, which was a blessing. I had plans to make things better. I would have a night partying to get out the feelings. It would be the perfect solution.

~

"*Y*ou ready for your shift tonight?" Riley asked.

"No. I haven't seen Drew since Sunday. Three days to stew on everything doesn't exactly feel the greatest, but I guess the good news is I'm at the bottom, so everything has to go up, right?"

Riley giggled. "Maybe. But I still think it would be pretty awkward. Like, do you act like the conversation didn't happen and nothing is wrong? Or do you try and interact with him more?"

I frowned. "Well, great. Now I'm overanalyzing it." I shut my locker and nearly choked.

Drew strolled toward my locker, hands in his pockets, gaze on the floor instead of ahead of him.

"Crap. He's right behind you."

Riley started to turn.

"No! Don't look. Pretend we're discussing something."

"We are talking about something."

I shoved her elbow. "Something *else*."

Riley rolled her eyes. "Fine. Are you sure you want to go to this party on Friday?"

"What? Of course I am. You're not backing out, are you?"

"No. I just—"

Drew stopped inches from where we stood. "Hey, Sophie." He nodded at Riley. "Hi, Riley, right?"

She nodded.

"Nice to meet you." His hands buried farther into his pockets. "I don't want to interrupt, but I didn't want you to worry, Sophie."

"Oh?"

"I won't be at the theater today. I had to change my shift last minute, so you'll work with Courtney. Mr. Martin already knows and cleared it. I just didn't want you to wonder. Yanno, after ..."

I nodded. "No problem. Thanks for letting me know."

"Sure." He combed his fingers through his hair. "Well, I must head out. See ya later."

"See you."

Riley waved then turned to me. "Well, that was interesting. Do you really think it had nothing to do with your conversation?"

I shrugged. "No idea. At least I don't have to worry how he will react though."

"Very true. You ready to go?"

I nodded and tossed my bookbag over my shoulder; at least one night could go well for me, hopefully.

~

A few hours later, Riley dropped me off at the theater for my shift. The air felt lighter somehow, even though the heat increased every day. Soon it would be stifling from the humidity, but I didn't mind.

Courtney waited for me by the snack counter and waved as she saw me walk through the doorway. She sprinted toward me. "Hey, rookie."

"Hello."

Courtney laughed. "Just kidding, but that could be catchy. Rookie Soph. What do you think?"

"Hmm. I don't know."

Courtney waved her hand in front of her face. "No worries. I'm pumped to have someone shadow me. Are you ready?"

I chuckled. "Someone is very cheery today."

"You're my first shadow. I'm excited to show Mr. Martin what I can do." She winked at me. "Maybe I'll even get you stolen from Drew if it's shocking enough."

I raised my left shoulder. "Possibly."

"Today we are reprising our roles behind the snack counter. But it's a Wednesday night, so we generally don't have a crazy number of moviegoers. It's usually pretty slow."

"Gotcha. Will I still be on popcorn?"

"Yep. If we have time, I might show you my end a little too, but popcorn for the most part."

"Sounds good. I'll grab my headset from the staff lounge and be right out."

When I returned, Courtney was carrying box after box behind the counter.

"Can I help?"

"Absolutely. Grab a box and bring it back. We have a few left to grab, then we need to unpack and restock."

My eyes widened. "These are all snacks?"

She nodded. "Crazy, right?"

"Yeah. How often do we restock?"

"Every few days or so. Depends on the rush and what they go for. You can guarantee to always restock Sour Patch Kids or cookie dough bites. Some of the others are less sought after."

"Wow. I never thought about that."

Courtney chuckled. "The joys of the theater industry. You'll learn all kinds of things."

"I'm sure I will. Where's your favorite station to work?"

"Probably at the snack counter. You never know what kind of night it will be, and you can interact with them."

"That makes sense. I would just get so hungry being around the food all the time."

"After you make enough popcorn and, let's be honest, eat enough in a short amount of time, you get over it. There are times I really want it, but it loses its draw."

"I can't imagine not wanting popcorn all the time."

"Give it a few weeks, and I'll ask you again."

"If I make it the next few weeks."

Courtney's brows drew together. "Why wouldn't you?"

"I don't know. Drew isn't thrilled to have me shadow him. Who knows, I guess."

"I don't see that at all. You've done well, and he's the first to admit that."

"Really?"

She nodded. "Whatever baggage you two have, he's not someone to bring it to work. He's not like that. Keeps things super separate. If you did something bad at work, maybe that would be different, but I can't see you doing that."

"That's good to know."

"Were you worried you might not make it out of the trial period?"

I shrugged. "I suppose so. Mr. Martin sounds very serious about everything. I guess I always have that wonder if I don't do well. Plus, I really like working here and the distraction it gives me from being home. Losing that would suck."

"I understand that. My parents aren't very hands-on. They do their own thing, which sounds great, but it gets boring so fast. Not to mention, we don't have much money, and this let me earn money for what I wanted and not have to ask them. What's your family like?"

"It's just my mama and my brother. My dad died almost six years ago, but Mama started dating. It's not exactly what I hoped for, so avoiding it sounds like the best option right now."

"Don't like the guy?"

"It's not really that. He seems fine. He's just not my dad."

"Gotcha. Well, good luck with that, but I think you'll be around here for a while. At least as long as you want to be."

"I hope so."

"No hope about it. Drew won't let you fail." Courtney stacked the empty boxes and walked toward the back doors.

Could she be right? Would Drew really keep our personal stuff separate? It meant we would see each other a lot more and consistently. Did that mean he was okay with the idea? Or was he just being nice?

I moved to my spot behind the popcorn maker and checked what I needed to do. Dwelling on the what-ifs wouldn't help me solve anything anyway.

CHAPTER 11

The clothing options for the party were sprawled across my bed while Riley rummaged through my shoes.

"What are you looking for?" I asked.

"I don't know. I don't have many cute shoes. I wear sneakers and boots sometimes. It's nice and warmer outside. I need, like, cute wedges or something."

"Hmm, I don't know if I have any that would look like right with your outfit. You need, like, brown wedges to go with your capris. I only have white ones, I think."

She sighed. "Darn."

"I think your shoes are fine, stop worrying. Besides, you already have the guy on the hook. He won't be worried about what shoes you're wearing."

Riley rolled her eyes. "I don't have *the guy* on the hook. You know Randy and I are just friends, no dating."

"Honestly, do you two repeat it to convince us or to convince yourselves? You kiss and go on *dates*; how is that not being more than friends?"

"We haven't kissed that many times," she said as she

twisted the laces of a pair of my shoes around her finger. "We're friends who care a lot about each other."

"If you say so, but it sure looks like more to everyone else. It's not a bad thing if you guys like each other and want to be together. It's been months since you found out about his family."

"Yeah, I know, and I wish it didn't bother him. I don't care what happens with his dad, as long as he's okay. But as long as he wants to wait, I'm fine with that."

"Truly? You truly don't want to be more?"

Riley flopped onto my desk chair. "I don't know, Sophie. That's a hard question when I know that no matter what I want, things aren't there yet."

"True, but it's just us. Do you want to be *together*, together?"

Riley's cheeks reddened.

I chuckled. "I suppose that's my answer. Maybe he'll change his mind sooner than later. He'd be a fool to let you go just because things with his family aren't perfect. I understood the logic in the beginning. You two didn't really know each other well, but now? No way."

"Yeah, well. Let's stop discussing me." Riley stood and ran her fingers over the dresses on my bed. "I love this one."

The one in question was a strapless, turquoise sundress with a straight-across neckline and a sheath cut. It fell just above my knee and was my absolute favorite summer dress.

"I love it too, but I would freeze to death."

"Not really. It's been warmer lately. Throw a denim jacket over it and it'd be cute and warmer."

I tapped the hanger to my chin. "Hmm, that might work."

"Of course, it would. Shelby would be proud of my fashionable choice."

I giggled. "I don't know that I'd go that far. You are

nowhere near Shelby-stylish yet." I checked the time on my phone. "Speaking of, where is she?"

"She said she'd be here by seven-thirty. She still has time."

"Well, I'll get dressed then. I'll be right back."

Riley nodded as she scrolled through her phone.

I snatched the dress from my bed and strolled to Mama's closet. She had a better jean jacket than I did, and it would go with this color. Once I found it, I backtracked to the bathroom. I set the clothing on the back of the door and stared into the mirror. I didn't usually put on makeup, but tonight I wanted things to be different, feel different. Shelby had agreed to help, so why not?

It took me maybe five minutes to get dressed. I gathered the hangers and closed the door.

Caleb stood inches from my face as I turned around. He looked at me then scrunched his nose. "What are you doing? Why are you wearing that?"

I shoved past him. "None of your business, dweeb."

He gasped. "Are you going to a party?"

"So what if I am?" I said before shutting the door.

Why were little brothers so nosy? Most of the time he was engrossed in his videogames. Why did he have to take this minute to be attentive?

"Shelby just texted. She's pulling up."

"I'll go let her in."

I walked to the front door, hoping Caleb was nowhere to be seen. I opened the door just as Shelby stopped on the porch.

"Perfect timing," she said and eyed my outfit. "Oh, that's cute."

"Thanks. Partly Riley's idea. I love yours too. I could never pull that off though."

Shelby smoothed her deep-purple pencil skirt. Her flowy shirt was tucked in slightly in the front and complimented her skin tone. "You definitely could. You just don't like that style."

"True. I like it on you, just not me."

Shelby chuckled. "Exactly. Is Riley ready too?"

I nodded. "Should be only a few minutes after you apply my makeup."

"Works for me. Any ideas on what you want?"

"Not really. I guess whatever works with my outfit and doesn't make me stand out too much. I don't want to feel like it's caked on, you know?"

"Absolutely. I'll stay more neutral."

Shelby followed me to my bedroom.

Riley sat up. "Hey, Shelby. Love the skirt. You look amazing, such a shame Luke can't see you."

Shelby rolled her eyes. "Is Randy coming tonight?"

"Eventually. He has to finish his shift at Morgan's Market first, then he said he would swing by if we're still there."

"That'll be fun. Have you guys gone to a party together yet?"

Riley shook her head. "Just your Christmas ball."

Shelby cringed. "Man, that feels like forever ago. Well, I'd say you two are in need of a party then!"

I sat in my desk chair. "Does this seat work?"

Shelby nodded and rummaged through her makeup bag. She removed tubes and compacts and brushes I had no idea existed for makeup, let alone their purpose.

I closed my eyes and let her work.

"Speaking of needing a party," Riley said, "when will Luke be back? Is he coming for the spring festival?"

"No. He'll be home a week or so later for Easter, so he couldn't make both."

"I'm sorry, Shelby. That really stinks."

"It is what it is. I can't really change it, yanno?"

"Still, I can't imagine waiting that long to see if there was something between the both of you."

I raised my eyebrow.

"Hold still," Shelby said.

"Sorry, I was reacting to what Riley said. You really can't understand waiting that long? You and Randy are waiting to see if something is between you."

Riley exhaled. "Not really."

"How so?" Shelby asked.

"Because I know there's something between us. You and Luke haven't declared any feelings to each other. So, for all you know, you're both destined to be friends."

"That sounds really harsh," I said.

"No. That's not what I meant. I know how Randy feels. Shelby only knows how she feels. That's all."

Shelby giggled as she brushed powder over my eyelids. "I know what you meant, Riley. I agree, not to mention I don't know what I really want. January was so long ago. What's to say things are the same as they were when he left?"

"Do you two text still?" I asked.

"Most of the time, but it's just about our days. We don't really discuss anything important. We had deeper talks when he was here over break."

"Have you considered asking him what he thinks?" Riley asked.

"Possibly, but we're only a few weeks away from Easter. At this point, I'd rather wait and have any conversation like that in person." Shelby zipped something near my head. "All done. Check it out."

I spun on my chair until I faced the mirror by my dresser. I stood and walked closer. Shelby had kept the makeup natural. For the most part, I couldn't tell I was wearing anything except for the eyeliner, mascara, and the light-colored eyeshadow. Whatever she did, it worked with my reddish-brown hair and green eyes.

Shelby nibbled the corner of her lip. "What do you think?"

"I like it. I can't believe it's me. I look completely different."

Riley nodded. "You look good."

I clapped my hands. "Well, are we ready to go ladies?"

"Yes!" Riley shouted.

We filed from the bedroom and walked to Riley's car. This night was what I needed: time to relax and be with my friends.

~

Shelby walked Riley through the directions to Brian's house.

My palms were sweaty. I had never been to a high school party before, let alone one at the captain of the football team's house.

Riley pulled into a longer driveway that weaved through the trees. This house was in the back, secluded—the perfect location for a party. "Wow," Riley said as she parked the closest she could to the house. "This is insane. So many people are here already."

Shelby nodded. "This is pretty standard for a Brian party."

"Well, crap. We've been missing out, apparently," I said.

People from our high school and people I didn't recognize arrived. They hopped from their vehicles, boisterous and excited. It was like they had all been given the key ingredients to enter a party and we had been left out.

Shelby opened the door and straightened her skirt. She threw the strap of her purse over her shoulder and waited while the rest of us climbed from Riley's Impala. "So, normally, there would be a bonfire or something in the back of the house. Drinks are self-serve in the kitchen. Bathroom is in the hallway, second door on the right when we go in. Otherwise, just mingle. If anyone asks why you're there, just let them know you're with me." Shelby leaned closer. "I doubt they will. Lots of people crash these parties."

Riley gulped loudly. "Are we sure we want to do this?"

"Heck yes!" I shouted.

Two teenage boys near us stared and shook their heads.

"I'm pumped for tonight. I'm already feeling better. Let's go."

We followed Shelby into the house.

People were everywhere. Brian's house was a massive ranch-style home. The floors were a dark hardwood, while the walls were a light gray. Photos and picture frames lined the hallways and the mantle of the fireplace. A small, narrow hallway branched from the vestibule toward the back of the house. The family room, dining room, and kitchen were all open and fed into one another.

Most of the people were body to body, starting in the dining room. Furniture had been moved to the side to create a makeshift dancefloor.

"Wow," Riley said.

"You can say that again." I pushed through the crowd at the door and tried to find a place to stand. "This is nuts."

Shelby giggled. "Oh what partiers you two are."

Riley rolled her eyes. "That won't work. I'm quite comfortable in knowing that I don't miss this or feel left out in any way."

"You said drinks are in the kitchen, right, Shelby?" I asked.

She nodded.

I pushed through the dancing crowd and found a spot near the kitchen counters. The house would have been nice if everyone hadn't created a disaster scene from the party. Mama would have killed me to treat the house like this. Either Brian's parents didn't care or he had a really good way of hiding his parties. I found a keg in the kitchen and alcohol bottles. The smell of the beer turned up my nose, but something needed to take my edge off. "Any ideas?" I asked Shelby.

"I don't usually drink at these things. You could make a mixed drink or something though."

I stared at her as if she had suddenly taken flight. "You do remember who you're talking to, right? I haven't made a mixed drink before. I don't even know what I would add."

A guy I recognized as a senior stood in the kitchen corner. His name was Brad or Ben, I thought. He extended his hand to shake. "Hey, the name's Steve. Do you ladies need help?"

Oops, definitely not a Ben or Brad.

Riley's brows drew together. "I'm good."

Shelby shook her head.

I leaned against the counter and tilted my head to the right. "What do you have in mind, Steve?"

"I couldn't help but to hear your issue with what to drink. Could I recommend maybe a shot of tequila or vodka to start you off?"

I crinkled my nose. "I don't know about shots. I was thinking something simple."

Steve stroked his chin. "The simplest thing here is the beer."

The smell wafted to me and made me cringe at the thought, but if it was the simplest, what choice did I have? "Okay, Steve. Beer it is then."

He poured me a cup and handed it over. The top frothed with foam from pouring.

Riley placed her hand on my arm. "Are you sure you want to drink?"

I nodded, took a long swig and forced myself to swallow the slightly warm liquid. It wasn't great, but I could manage.

Riley and Shelby exchanged glances.

"I saw that. I'm fine, seriously. I just want to take the edge off. Don't worry about it, okay? Want to check out the back yard?"

"Sure. It's musty in here anyway," Shelby said and walked toward the French doors off the dining room.

Outside was just as busy as inside the house. In the center of the crowd was a large patio and fireplace. Brian stoked the fire with a large stick while the crowd cheered and raised their red cups.

"So, do we know anyone here well enough to have a conversation? Or are we just going to hang out on the fringes of the party?"

Riley shrugged. "It's your idea, so what do you want to do?"

"Let's sit by the fire on that empty bench."

We walked to the bench and sat.

I scanned the surroundings as I tried to figure out who everyone was. It was like a whole new world from classes. People I had never expected to be at Brian's party were here and looked like they were enjoying themselves. I had been missing out on a rite of passage for high school—something I was all too happy to rectify tonight.

Shelby and Riley whispered to each other about something. Normally, I would care and ask about it. But not tonight.

"I'm going to run in and go to the bathroom. Be right back," I said.

Riley started to stand. "Do you want me to come with you?"

"Nope. You two save the bench. I'll be back."

Riley watched me warily, but it was just a bathroom trip. It's not like I was going inside to dance or anything.

The crowd inside had doubled since we had moved to the back yard—a feat I didn't expect to be possible. Mere inches separated people as they swayed to the beat over the speakers. The hallway to the bathroom was slightly better but not by much.

I had to remember what door Shelby said it would be. *Think, Sophie.*

That's it! The bathroom was the second door on the right from the front door. I counted until I found the second door from the opposite direction. I knocked lightly, hoping I wouldn't have to wait to go to the bathroom.

No one answered.

I turned the knob and entered. I flipped on the light to reveal a lavender bathroom with dark gray accents throughout. It was a half bath and the perfect bathroom for guests, although clearly someone had already gotten sick in here. I shook my head and tried to focus on going to the bathroom and getting out. I didn't need to smell anyone else's puke for any length of time.

The door closed behind me and I nearly ran into someone standing directly in front of the bathroom door. "Oh, I'm sorry. It's all yours," I said.

"Hey, it's you from earlier," Steve said as he eyed my hands. "Where's your beer? You can't walk around empty handed."

"I left it with my friends."

"Well, here. Let's get you a fresh one."

"That's okay. I don't need one."

Steve flashed a wide grin. "It's just one more. I'm sure your cup is warm by now."

He was probably right.

I shrugged. "Okay. One more cup."

Steve smiled and nudged us through the crowd. He poured me another cup and himself one then handed it over. "So, where do you go to school?"

"Honey Cove High."

Steve's eyes widened. "No, not possible. I would have recognized you."

"I'm a junior, so probably not."

Steve stroked his chin. "I must have not been paying attention in the hallways then. You're too beautiful to not notice."

My cheeks blushed. "Thanks. I need to get back to my friends." I raised my cup toward him. "Thanks for the beer." I turned and walked to the French doors.

Steve grabbed my hand as I turned and pulled. "Wait. Why don't you stay for a dance?"

I looked from him to the door and back. "I really should go back so my friends don't worry."

"Just one dance." He puffed out his lower lip. "Please?"

"Okay, fine. Just once."

Steve grinned and guided me to the dance floor. The song that blared over the speakers was a pop song with a decent beat.

I, however, never danced. Not ever. Not for friends, not in groups. Never.

Steve swayed his hips to the beat and stared into my eyes.

I stood stalk still, unsure what to do.

Steve gently reached for my hips and moved them in time with the song and his. He wasn't pushy, but it still felt weird to be dancing with someone—especially a guy. Steve kept his hands on my waist as we moved together.

When the song ended, I exhaled and downed my cup. "Thanks for the dance."

"Of course, but it looks like you've got an empty cup again. Want a refill?"

I stared at the white bottom of the cup. I shook my head. "Nah. I'm heading back to my friends." I pulled away before Steve could realize what was happening.

The cool breeze outside set my senses on fire. Inside had been too hot and clustered; I felt free again outside.

Shelby and Riley stared at me as I approached. They looked slightly annoyed.

"Where have you been?" Riley asked. "We've been worried. You said you had to go to the bathroom."

"I did, then Steve caught me inside and asked me to dance. I did one song and then bolted back out here."

Shelby rose her eyebrow. "Steve asked you to dance? Interesting."

I cocked my head to the side. "Why do you say it like that?"

"No reason. He's just … well, just be careful with him. He has a reputation."

"I'm not going to go out with him. It was just a dance."

"I know. I'm just letting you know. I wouldn't want something to happen to you, is all."

I nodded and jolted when my phone buzzed. I pulled out my phone and saw the message from Mama. *Sophie, don't forget we're spending time with Rowan tomorrow. Please don't stay out too late.*

Seeing his name sent fire through my body. I didn't want to see Rowan, let alone hang out with him. Why couldn't she understand that? What was I supposed to do? Go to this activity and pretend we were a happy family? No, absolutely not.

I stood to go back inside to find Steve. Maybe I would have that third beer after all.

CHAPTER 12

I vaguely remembered Randy arriving after twenty minutes, maybe? I wasn't sure if it was twenty minutes or not.

Riley and Shelby ran to check on me when I abruptly went back into the party, but I explained I wanted to dance and that they needed to relax.

Steve was easy to find, hovering in the kitchen near the keg. He smiled wide when he saw me and gestured toward it.

I nodded, and he poured me another beer. We pushed back to the dancefloor, and I let loose.

Then things went dark.

I now stared, blinking away the blurriness of what I thought was the bathroom, as I lay on the floor. My head pounded, and I could vaguely hear someone whispering my name as they softly stroked my hair.

What on earth was going on?

The blurry person resembled what I thought Riley had been wearing, but things didn't look right with her face.

"Riley? Is that you?" I asked.

The blurry person jolted. "Yes! Sophie, you're awake. Oh my god. Are you okay?"

I tried to sit upright and things spun. "What?" I covered my ears. "Why are you yelling?"

"Sophie, you're drunk. We need to get you home."

"What? I am not. I had, like, two beers."

"No, you didn't. You had way more than that. I have no idea how many, but you're hammered. You passed out while dancing. Steve just left you on the floor. Thank god Shelby saw you and dragged you in here with the help of some boys." Riley shuffled around me, causing the noise to echo through my ears and body like a ricochet.

Then I heard muffled talking.

"Yeah, she's awake."

"She has no idea."

"I won't."

"Please hurry."

I grimaced as I tried to sit upright again. "Riley, what are you doing? Let's leave this bathroom. I don't want to lay here anymore."

"When Randy and Shelby come back, we'll help move you."

"Pshhh. I don't need help," I slurred. I was fine. Everyone was overreacting.

The door opened wide, spilling the noise from the party into the small, cramped room.

I slammed my hands over my ears. "Turn down that noise! What are they doing out there?"

Riley eyed the open doorway. "See? Help me move her."

A blurry Shelby and Randy moved closer to me.

"We're going to put our hands under your arms and lift at the same time. Okay, Sophie? Just try to keep your legs straight," Randy said.

"I'm fine. The room is just moving a bit. Probably the

aftershock from the music." I felt the pressure of their hands under my arms, and they lifted. I felt like I was floating, until the whole room went around and around like a merry-go-round. "Wow. Who spun the room?" My feet and legs felt like Jell-O. Why couldn't I walk like I normally did? The cool air blew over my face as we walked. "Wait, why are we leaving the party?"

Riley patted my arm. "It's time to go, Sophie. We're all leaving."

My arms flailed around my body. "No! I don't want to. I'm having so much fun. This is the best night of my life."

"Sophie, you don't know what you're saying. Let us get you to Riley's car and take you home," Shelby said.

The door to Riley's Impala creaked open as they set me in the back seat. The plushy seats felt like a nice fuzzy carpet. I scooted across the seat and laid sprawled out.

Voices outside the car floated to me in random order.

"It's fine. I don't mind."

"I owe you, Randy."

"Get a buckle around her even if she's laying down."

"You must tell her mom."

"Thanks."

"I'll text when we get her there."

I wanted to fight against their words, but the seat enveloped me too much. I had no more strength. I gave in and let my eyelids flutter close. I would fight later. For now, I would sleep. Sleep was good.

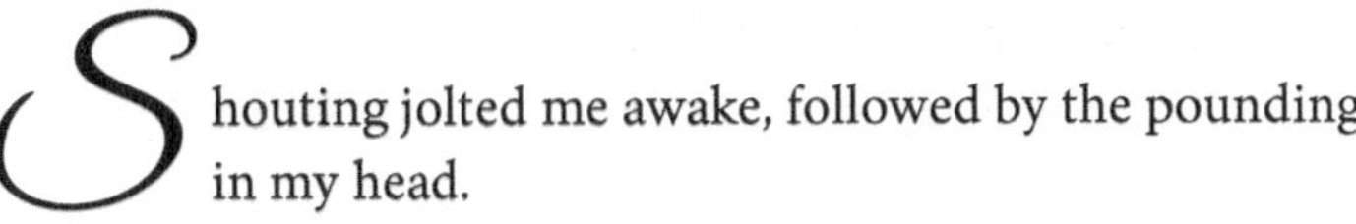

*S*houting jolted me awake, followed by the pounding in my head.

What the hell?

I rubbed my temples, hoping it released the pressure.

What was wrong with my head? I struggled to remember anything that would give me a clue to my condition.

The sun streamed through the blinds and curtains in my bedroom. It was daytime?

What about … oh no. The party.

I winced as I tried to sit upright. The pounding in my head intensifying. I doubled over and felt absolutely awful.

I needed to find my phone and figure out what had happened.

But who was shouting? Maybe something to wake me up would help.

I practically rolled off the edge of my bed, which turned out to be a horrible idea. The room spun, and my stomach lurched. Yeah, definitely don't think last night went well.

The shouting became louder, and I realized Mama was calling my name over and over again.

Well, damn.

The trek to my door was god awful. I almost heaved twice, and the room spun so frequently I had to hold onto something to keep from falling over. Whatever Mama needed, this would not go well.

I found her sitting at the kitchen table, drinking something from a mug. She peered at me from over the side of her mug. "I see someone is finally awake!" she shouted.

I winced. Why was she talking so loudly?

"Ah, yes. The lovely effects of drinking—a hangover."

I froze midway to the kitchen chair opposite her. My mouth hung open, my eyes widened.

"Oh, yes. I know you drank last night. I figured you wouldn't remember Riley bringing you home after she had called me." She wagged her finger at me. "How could you act so stupid last night?"

"I-I …"

"Nope. I'm not done. Sit." She shoved a bottle of Gatorade

and a few acetaminophen tablets toward me. "Take these." She waited for me to swallow the pills and take a few swigs. "Do you understand that if it wasn't for your friends, something terrible could have happened to you? I have never known you to be so irresponsible, but man, you sure nailed it last night. Someone could have taken advantage of you in your state. Or you could have ended up in someone else's car." She held her head in her hands. "I can't even bear to think of all the ways last night could have gone wrong. You are royally grounded, Sophie. From now until I stop being angry or two weeks, whichever one is longer."

"I'm sorry, Mama."

She raised her hand. "Save it, Sophie. I'm not in the mood to hear anything from you right now. In a few hours, Rowan is coming over to take us to miniature golf. You are going."

My eyes widened.

"Yep. Hungover or not, you're going. So go lay down, pull it together, because by one o'clock, you better be dressed and ready to go. You are walking such a thin line that you better be on your perfect behavior with Rowan today too. No moodiness, sighing, or rolling your eyes when you think I can't see you. Or so help me."

"Okay. I get it. I'll be ready."

She nodded and waved me from the room.

I snatched the Gatorade from the table and leaned against the hallway as I slid to my room. This was not how I wanted to spend my Saturday morning. I plopped into my bed and barely moved until I had set an alarm on my phone for 11:30. Hopefully by then I would feel a little better.

～

The sound of my alarm jolted me awake, then the drowsiness and spinning resumed. My room didn't appear to be spinning quite as badly as before, but I could still tell the effects lingered in my system. I rubbed my eyes and forehead. What had I been thinking? I had wanted to only take the edge off. I didn't want to get drunk.

I silenced my phone's alarm and checked my messages. I had a few from Shelby and Riley in the group text.

Riley: *How are you feeling this morning? I hope you're okay. I'm sorry I told your mom, but we were so worried. Text me when you can.*

Shelby: *Remember to drink a lot of fluids and take it slow. It won't feel much better for a while. Food like eggs and other light things should help too. Let us know how you are when you get these.*

The guilt slammed into me as I read their messages. I could tell they were worried, and why shouldn't they be? I had acted irresponsibly and out of character. I should have known better than to drink so much at that party.

I shot off a reply to let them know I was okay. *I'm up. Super hungover. Mama is pissed. I have to go to miniature golf today with everyone ... including Rowan. I feel so awful I don't even care. Thank you for getting me home safely. Don't worry. I would have told your parents too.*

I stowed the phone on the nightstand and gathered my outfit for the day—jean capris and a mint-green three-quarter length shirt. I peeked through the doorway to see if anyone was in the hallway. Luckily, it was vacant.

I scurried to the bathroom and locked the door. I filled the bathroom with steam from the shower and waited until it covered the mirror to get in. The heat from the water seeped into my pores. It relaxed my muscles, tight from the stress of what Mama would do.

I scrubbed at my skin until it was bright pink and toweled off. I had no energy to attempt makeup or do much besides brush my teeth and hair. I gathered my dirty clothes and walked to my bedroom.

I still had a little over an hour before we would leave, but I didn't want to be late. There was absolutely no way Mama would go easy on me for how I felt. If anything, I had to prepare for it to be the worst experience of my life—not just because of how I felt but that I would have to pretend nothing was wrong with me.

My stomach grumbled. I had forgotten I really hadn't eaten since last night. I meandered to the kitchen. I rummaged through the refrigerator and cabinets, trying to find something that would fill me up but wouldn't make me want to puke my guts out.

I settled on making a peanut butter and jelly sandwich and a side of apple slices. I brought my meal to the kitchen table and slowly ate. The first bite felt like shoving down food after having the stomach bug, but I pushed on, and eventually, it didn't feel so awful to eat.

I grabbed another Gatorade and sucked it down. It surprisingly made me feel better quicker than I had thought possible. I brought my plate to the couch. The remote was on the counter, and I used it to flip through channels. I landed on the HGTV channel and absorbed myself into the episode until the sound of footsteps startled me.

Caleb bounded down the hallway toward me. He plopped on the couch near me. "Whatcha watching?"

It took everything not to shout at him or be rude. He was loud, and the bouncing caused my stomach to do flips. "HGTV."

"Cool."

I stared at him. Why was he so chipper? Thankfully, that was the last time he really talked until Mama strolled out to show us her outfit. She wore dark jeans, a flowery top, and a light cardigan.

"What do you think?"

Caleb's eyebrows rose. "Looks good, Mama."

I nodded.

She smiled and checked her wristwatch. "He should be here in five minutes. Both of you go use the bathroom."

Caleb stood and sprinted to the bathroom first.

I took a much slower approach and shut off the TV first before heading in that direction.

Mama stood in front of me, blocking my path. "How are you feeling?"

"So-so. I ate a peanut butter and jelly sandwich and had one more Gatorade. It's helped a little more."

"I'll give you another dose of acetaminophen before we leave. Go ahead and use my bathroom. You know how long your brother takes."

I nodded and opened her door. I couldn't figure out how I was being setup, but I knew it had to be coming. She had been so mad earlier, but now she was being nice—thoughtful even.

I hurried into her room and went to the bathroom. I checked my face in the mirror. The bags under my eyes were puffy, and I had a deep circle with darker coloring. I looked rough, but at least no one from school would see me like this.

No one else waited in the family room, so I sat on the couch just as someone knocked on the door.

Mama jogged to the door and patted her hands on her jeans before she opened it. Her smile widened as she saw Rowan.

He walked through the doorway and gave her a quick hug before passing her a bouquet of flowers. "These are for you." Then he brought a smaller bouquet of daisies to me on the couch. "And these are for you."

My eyes widened. He brought me flowers?

"Thanks," I said as I walked to the kitchen to find a vase and put them in water. Mama could cut them when we got home, but I didn't feel like doing it right then.

Mama entered the kitchen shortly after I had placed the bouquet in water. "That was so thoughtful he brought us both flowers."

I nodded but then remembered Mama wanted my best behavior and no grumbling. I had to do more, or she would tack on time to my sentence. "It's very kind."

Mama smelled her flowers. Her bouquet had been light pink and red roses. Her eyes twinkled with delight.

We returned to the living room together where Caleb and Rowan seemed to be joking about something.

"Shall we head out?" Mama asked.

Rowan held open the door for us all.

Mama locked up, and we filed into his SUV. This felt so similar to last time that huge amounts of déjà vu hit me hard. That coupled with the still lingering effects of my hangover didn't do much to settle my stomach.

The ride to Bud's Miniature Golf didn't take long. It was only a few blocks outside the town limits. I hadn't been to Bud's in years, since … well, since my father had died. My gut twisted, and I suppressed the feeling. I couldn't have those kinds of feelings today. I had agreed to be on my best behavior, and that's what I would do.

There was a short line at the front. Rowan paid for us all, to Mama's chagrin. She didn't like feeling someone else was taking care of us, not since Dad.

I chose my club and a purple ball, Caleb chose green, and Mama chose orange, while Rowan chose black.

The courses at Bud's were either Around the World themed or Cowboy themed. Rowan went cowboy. Personally, I didn't care either way. It would be eighteen holes of torture as I forced my body to exert energy it clearly didn't have and to be around company I couldn't be honest about how I felt.

Mama pulled a Gatorade from her purse and handed it to me while Rowan and Caleb walked forward to scope out the first hole. "Take this and drink some. Here's your acetaminophen too. You look so pale."

"Thanks, Mama."

"Don't thank me just yet. Eighteen holes in the sun, even during the spring, can make you want to die. But at least you should be hydrated."

I smiled weakly. I couldn't tell if she was trying to be humorous or just stating things matter-of-factly. Either way, I would take anything she offered, because she was right; I felt terrible.

Rowan went first, followed by Caleb, Mama, and then me for each hole. It let me watch how each of them putted prior and hopefully would let me rest in between. It didn't feel like much of a rest, to be honest. I felt lousy and was playing horribly. At the first hole, my ball bounced off the large cowboy boot and nearly hit my head.

Rowan stifled his laugh while Caleb exaggeratedly rolled on the ground and died from laughter, gripping his sides as he bellowed. The noise and energy exerted just made me feel worse.

Mama thankfully let me stay silent most of the game as we putted around the holes.

It wasn't until the tenth hole when Rowan asked me a question directly. "Sophie, you're friends with Shelby right?"

I nodded, regretting the motion instantly.

"Are you planning to help her with the spring festival next weekend?"

I looked at Mama, wondering how to answer. I had

planned to help her, but with my current grounding, I wasn't sure what I was allowed to do anymore.

"She is," Mama spoke up.

My eyes widened.

"It's a wonderful opportunity, and she did promise to help her," Mama added.

Ah, so that was her reasoning. If I hadn't already been counted on to help, Mama would never have agreed to let me go now.

"Yes. I'm excited to help. She's been working on it for months now. I hope it goes well for her."

Rowan smiled. "She's a Rowe; I have no doubt. She's been asking to see the marketing details a lot lately, so I've gotten to know her a little bit. She's a really nice young lady."

"She has turned out to certainly be a good friend."

Rowan focused on Caleb gearing up to swing his club. The hole had a large cowboy in the middle whose foot moved back and forth to cover the chute that would take it to the hole. Timed well, it was a guaranteed hole in one.

Rowan called out to Caleb, "Wait! Don't hit it in that direction."

It was too late. Caleb nailed the ball, and it ricocheted off the cowboy's foot, past the green for the course, and straight into Caleb's groin.

I nearly choked as I watched the perfect timing.

Mama dropped her club and ran to Caleb. "Are you okay?"

Caleb grunted as he laid on the ground.

The giggles erupted from my mouth even though I tried to push them down.

Soon Mama and then Rowan joined in.

Caleb glowered at us all. "It's not funny."

"It so *is*!"

Rowan chuckled then covered his mouth with his hand. "Let me help you up."

Caleb slowly climbed to his feet and stared at his golf ball. "Stupid thing," he said as he kicked it with his toe.

"This isn't the major leagues. You don't need to swing so hard, Caleb," Mama said.

"I was just trying to give it enough force to get to the hole."

"You gave it plenty of force," I said.

Caleb glared while Mama covered her mouth as she hid her smile. But I could tell she smiled anyway from the crinkle by her eyes.

"Why don't you try again but with less force," Rowan suggested.

Caleb grabbed his ball and set it on the center dot at the top of the course. He grabbed his club from the side where it landed when he had collapsed.

I inhaled as he swung again.

This time, the ball went through the chute and down to the lower level. Caleb peered over the edge and jumped. "Hole in one!"

Mama wiggled her finger. "Oh no. Hole in two. You have to count the first stroke."

I giggled. "Someone came to win."

Mama held her hands to the sky. "What? He hit the ball twice."

Rowan's right eyebrow rose. "Competitive, I see."

Mama shrugged.

The rest of the holes went smoother. I had even almost forgotten my hangover, although too quick of a jerk one way or the other caused the pounding in my head to rear its ugly head. But otherwise, the wobbliness had faded, and my balanced returned.

I had lost, which was no surprise. Rowan won, followed

by Mama, and then Caleb. It hadn't been too bad, but I certainly didn't plan to have a repeat anytime soon.

I wanted to crawl into my bed and watch TV until it was time for me to sleep. Maybe eat dinner somewhere in there too. Luckily, Rowan drove us home after the game and Mama agreed to let me do just that.

She brought me chicken noodle soup and another Gatorade, but otherwise, she left me alone to my own devices—a compromise I was grateful for. Tomorrow I would have to work, but until then, I enjoyed every minute to myself.

CHAPTER 13

I still felt horrible the following afternoon while I dressed for work. Somehow, even with the copious amounts of liquid and sleep, my body still revolted against my actions from Friday night. I stretched, trying to convince my muscles to relax after the abuse they had endured.

Mama waited for me in the family room. "You ready to leave? You don't want to be late."

I nodded.

"Caleb, your sister and I are leaving! I'll be back after I drop her off. Please keep the doors locked!"

I moseyed to Mama's SUV and hopped in the front seat.

Mama lowered the radio and pulled out of the driveway. "So, how's the theater been for you? Going well?"

"Yeah. Everyone is pretty nice."

"That's great, Sophie. I must say I wasn't keen on you getting a job for the reasons that pushed you to get one, but it is nice to have you focus on something after school for a few hours. I hope it keeps you in line with your responsibilities." She cleared her throat. "Any noteworthy coworkers?"

"Just Drew and Courtney so far. I don't really interact with anyone else. They're the only ones who do similar jobs as me."

"Well, that's certainly a start."

I nodded. This felt like a trap. It had been too soon for her to compliment me after royally screwing up on Friday. What was I missing?

"You did well yesterday during miniature golf. I don't think Caleb really noticed anything wrong."

"He never notices anything unless it has to do with videogames or food."

Mama giggled. "Not always true."

I raised my eyebrow. "Yes, true. He wouldn't notice it unless you ignited a neon sign on fire."

"Well, regardless, I'm thankful you kept to your word."

Did she think I had a choice? If I ever wanted to breathe fresh air again, then of course I had to do what she asked.

"Rowan knew, of course."

My jaw slackened. "You told him?"

"Yes. Why wouldn't I? He needed to know what the deal was, especially if you passed out from your hangover." She shook her head. "It certainly wasn't something I had expected to tell him though."

"I didn't exactly plan it."

Mama faced me. "Are you sure? You've been acting out a lot lately."

"I'm sure, Mama. I didn't plan to get wasted at the party. I just wanted … I just wanted some fun."

I couldn't tell her I wanted to release the tension Rowan brought into my life. Or how much the ache in my chest grew because he was replacing my father.

"I think you certainly blew past fun. Not to mention the pounding in your head from the hangover will probably be a lasting *fun*."

"Ha-ha. You win."

"I don't want to win. I just wish I understood what was going on with you more."

Thankfully, Mama pulled into the parking lot. I gathered my belongings and practically jumped from the moving SUV before Mama finished her thought.

"Thank you for driving me. I should be done by five. Can you pick me up?"

Mama nodded and waved as I walked backward toward the door.

When she pulled away, I walked through the front doors, finally able to relax. For once, I didn't feel the gnawing guilt in the pit of my stomach as I searched for Drew. Maybe things could get better now that I'd had my setback.

Drew scrolled through a handheld device as he stood by the ticket podium.

"Hey, Drew."

Drew looked up and smiled.

He actually smiled! An action I thought his face had forgotten to do when he was near me.

"Hey, Sophie. You ready? You'll be shifting all around today. It's kind of a crazy one. Courtney is out, so between you and me, we'll be oscillating between the snack counter and here. Think you can handle it?"

I nodded. "I'll get my headset and hurry back."

He gave me a thumbs up and refocused on the line that had formed at his podium.

By the time I had returned, he had shortened the queue to the last elderly couple who needed their tickets scanned. Once the couple left, he attended to me. "Did Courtney teach you any of the other stations for the snack counter?"

I shook my head. "I helped to restock the candy and snacks, but machine-wise, I was only on the popcorn maker."

He stroked his chin. "Okay, let's do this. Stay here, and in an hour or so, when someone else comes in, we'll switch you to the snack counter again and have you learn a few of the other stations. Sound good?"

"Works for me."

Drew patted my shoulder and walked to the snack counter.

Weird goosebumps erupted on my shoulder from the draft. I shivered from the goosebumps and focused on the podium. I didn't have a line yet, but I knew that could change at any second, and I wanted to be prepared.

~

Shelby arrived halfway through my shift.

"What are you doing here?" I asked.

Shelby carried a stack of card stock with writing over them. She plopped it onto the counter closest to the door. "These are for the spring festival. Today starts the scavenger hunts, for a lack of a better word. Anyone can receive one from any place participating. They get their card punched, and at each new participating diner, store, or theater, they receive another hole punch."

"Oh, that sounds like a lot of work."

"Yes and no. Handing them out, yes. Collecting them, yes. But in the meantime, while it happens, not so much."

"But wait, I thought it was only for businesses in Honey Cove?"

"Mostly. This is the only theater for us, and a few other businesses outside the city limits are in similar circumstances. Plus, why not do neighboring towns in sparse quantities? It encourages those towns to visit Honey Cove to participate."

I stared at one of the cards, surveying the businesses who

were participating. "This is really cool, Shelby. You and Randy came up with this?"

She nodded. "Can you point me in the direction of someone in charge? I gotta drop this stack off and head to the next location. I have at least ten more stops today."

I surveyed the lobby for Mr. Martin. When I couldn't find him, I went looking for Drew. "I'll be right back."

"Okay. I'll be waiting."

Drew was behind the snack counter and was the easiest to find.

"Do you know where Mr. Martin is?"

Drew scratched his head. "I haven't seen him in a few hours. Maybe he went to his office. Why?"

"Shelby has the pile of punch cards for Honey Cove's spring festival. I figured he would want to handle that."

"Yeah, you're probably right. I'll radio him with my headset."

Duh! Why didn't I think to use the headset?

Drew spoke in hushed tones into the small mic attached to his shirt. "Okay, should be out any minute."

"Thanks. I'll let Shelby know."

"Then can you come to the snack counter? I'll have you finish your shift with me."

I nodded and returned to Shelby. "Mr. Martin is the manager. He'll be out in a few minutes."

Shelby looked past me. "Who were you talking to?"

I rolled my eyes. "You and I both know I was talking to Drew."

Shelby's eyed widened. "Oh, was that him? You know it's so difficult to tell when you're that far away." She tilted her head. "How are things today with him?"

"They're fine. I need to go work. Good luck with your deliveries." I practically sprinted to the snack counter before Shelby could respond. It wasn't the time or place to be nosy about my interactions with Drew. She could wait until school, like everyone else.

"Okay, so I thought we could have you manage the nachos and cheese, pretzels and cheese, and the soda machines. What do you think?"

I nodded. "Works for me."

"Now most likely, you won't have to restock too many times since it's a Sunday, but on our busiest days, these items fly off the racks." Drew pointed to the hidden shelves behind the counter. "We keep the materials for the snacks here. Behind you is the warmer for the cheese if they choose to have it more than room temperature. Never put it in the microwave or it will burn them and explode all over."

I nodded, hoping that all the information he spewed at me would stick.

"The chips for nachos and cheese are in bags under the counter, and in the mini freezer, we have the pretzels we warm up in the microwave. Only make one or two pretzels for the racks at a time. You can always have more chips, because they last longer, but you don't want super cold pretzels, or they'll complain."

"Okay, and the soda machines?"

"Soda machines are fairly self-service, except when it needs to be changed. Otherwise, check there are still straws, lids, and cups after every large rush. If it's a day like today, check it every thirty minutes."

"Okay. I think I can manage that."

Drew nodded. "I'll be down on the popcorn end, and since today is a slower rush, if you need help, just let me know, and I can step in."

"Thanks. My only question is where are the straws, lids, and cups?"

"Good point. They're underneath the soda machine's cabinet. We keep the key right underneath here." He pointed to a bright orange taped key under the top counter. "Make sure to put it back when you're finished."

"Got it. Alright, let me get to work."

Drew smirked.

"What?"

He shook his head. "Nothing. I just never in my life expected to work with you like this."

"Is that a good thing or a bad thing at this point?"

He stroked his chin. "Too soon to tell. Things just got back on a normal course."

"Fair enough."

He walked to the popcorn machine as he rubbed the back of his neck.

I couldn't shake the feeling that something was different about the way he had said that, almost as if he had more to say but just wouldn't.

Oh well, all that mattered at this point was succeeding at my job.

$\mathcal{B}$oxes surrounded the front entrance to Shelby's guesthouse. I surveyed the house that seemed almost larger than my own house, yet this was for guests. I couldn't imagine having this much money in my family. We lived frugally and didn't have frills, but this, this was massive and wasn't even their house.

"Why are you waiting outside?" Riley asked.

"I'm just taking it all in. I've never seen the Rowe estate. This is nuts."

"Right? I couldn't believe it either until I saw it a month or so ago. It eats my apartment in New York."

"It eats my house here!"

She giggled. "Well, let's go in. From the look of the outside, I can't imagine the hustle and bustle inside."

I nodded and followed Riley as she knocked once and entered the hallway. The floors were a white tile, with the walls painted a light gray, almost white. Every inch was decorated with high maintenance design in mind. It was a long cry from our rancher.

"Hello?" Riley asked and peered around corners. "Sophie and I are here to help."

"We're back here. Follow the hallway and turn right," Shelby said.

Each room we passed on the way to that room was themed. From what I could tell, three bedrooms were on this level, with a front sitting room right off the front entrance.

Randy and Shelby sat in a circle surrounded by boxes, ribbons, wicker baskets, and plastic.

My eyes widened. "Holy crap. You weren't kidding."

Randy's short-sleeve shirt looked stretched and disheveled.

"How long have you two been at this?" Riley asked.

Shelby slid her finger over her phone to check the time. "Since school ended, so a few hours, but we were up late last night too."

Randy combed his fingers through his hair. "Every time we make progress, more supplies are delivered. It's nuts."

I found a cleared-off corner to the right of their chaos and sat. "What exactly are you preparing here?"

"Mostly baskets right now. They'll be auctioned off, and the proceeds will go to the companies, as well as to fund the festival itself. We have more baskets than we expected. Some companies offered to do a basket entirely themselves and also to go halfway in on another basket too. We have forty baskets to assemble now."

Riley gasped. "Wow. Why didn't the companies do it?"

Shelby snorted. "Those men wanted nothing to do with it that would take time. The way we got most of them to agree was only if they donated their product and we assembled it. If they had to do it, we probably would have had far less donations."

"Well, I'm not *great* with decorations and stuff, but I'll do whatever you need me to do," I said.

Randy checked the legal pad between him and Shelby. "Part of our issue is the boxes keep arriving, and we must unpack and sort. If you and Riley can help us unpack—they *should* be boxed in congruence with the basket they need to go in—that would be the most help. Then Shelby and I can assemble the basket once we know what we have."

Shelby nodded. "I'd rather find out if we have enough supplies now than when it gets too late and we run out of something to package up the donations."

I stood and pulled Riley to the edge of the room where the boxes were stacked over my head. "Consider it done."

Riley's eyes widened. "This will take forever," she muttered.

I shrugged. "Best get to it then." I faced Shelby. "Where are the boxcutters or scissors? Also, where do you want the unboxed materials to go when we're finished?"

Shelby tapped her pointer finger to her mouth, almost like she was telling someone to hush. "Let's organize it by company. Use the bedrooms and sitting rooms on this floor to organize it. Then we can see how much they have and how to split it between the baskets that are joint and separate."

I nodded.

Shelby stood and handed Riley and me both a pair of scissors and a boxcutter. "Thanks. I know you didn't have to do this. I do appreciate your time."

Riley shooed Shelby. "Please. That's what friends do."

Randy met Riley's gaze and winked.

I stared at the looming boxes. "Help me move this box to the floor. I can't quite reach the top."

Riley grabbed one side, and I grabbed the other underneath. We gently lowered it to the ground. I checked the shipping label on the box. The rest of the boxes in that stack all appeared to be from the same company. I grabbed the end of the box and moved it into the hallway. I pushed the first bedroom's door farther open and set the box inside. Once I had the whole stack in the room, I would open them all up.

Riley decided on a similar system. Soon the stack in the room Shelby and Randy were in was cleared.

The first box I opened contained lip balms, lotions, lipsticks, and other cosmetic products made from beeswax. Box after box contained more products made from bees. I flattened the boxes and collected the plastic it was packaged in and set it out front in a pile.

Riley joined me outside and sighed. "This is going to take forever."

I smirked. "Nah. I've got an idea."

Riley's eyebrow rose. "Do tell."

"Let's have a race."

She rolled her eyes. "A race? Sophie, we can't run right now. That won't help us."

"No, a race with the boxes. Whoever finishes getting their side in and into a bedroom wins. Then the loser opens the boxes."

Riley tapped her chin. "Deal."

I grinned. "You get that side. I'll get this side."

Riley silently counted the number of boxes on each side. When she seemed satisfied it was even, she nodded.

"Three."

"Two."

"One."

"Go!"

We launched into the boxes and hauled them inside. Every time I went for a new one, I checked how her side looked. For now, it seemed even. I had to beat her. Not only would it lessen how many boxes I opened, but it would feel nice to win.

I finally went outside to grab my last box but saw Riley there with a smug expression. "What? No way! Already?"

She crossed her arms and smirked. "Yep. You get to open the boxes."

I sighed and trudged back to the rooms. Boxes were everywhere, and it felt like an insurmountable task.

Riley followed in behind me on the first bedroom.

"What are you doing?"

"I might have won, but they need the boxes opened. I'll still help. I thought we could do one room together at a time then move on."

"That'd be nice to have some company."

"I agree."

We both grabbed a box from the stack, sat on the floor and pried them open.

"Randy looked ragged," I said.

She nodded. "He's been staying up late and working a lot this week. So much is riding on it for his family's company. I just hope it goes well and he can relax a little."

"He has so many responsibilities. It's insane."

"I know. I wish he had more people to help him."

"He has you, Riley. I'm sure that helps him tremendously."

"I try, but I don't know anything about the stresses of being a founding family and the company. I only know normal high school stuff. How am I supposed to support him on the things I know nothing about?"

"Just do what you're doing. If he needed more, I feel like he'd be the person to ask. You have to just be waiting for when he does."

She exhaled loudly. "I suppose."

"But ...?"

"But I don't know. Shelby and Randy have worked so hard together lately. What if he realizes I'm not the right fit for this world?"

"Please. He deeply cares about you. Shelby isn't interested in him like that, and I know Randy isn't into her like that."

"I know that. I do, but the thoughts still creep in."

"Is it because of how long things have been stalled?"

Riley averted her gaze and shuffled items around the box. "I guess. I don't really know what it is. Shelby has transformed so completely; what if he realizes she is what he needs in his world? She understands that part of his life better than I do. She lives it every day."

I scooted closer and rubbed her shoulder. "Randy is very clearly into you. He might be friends with Shelby, and they might understand those dynamics, but he chooses to bring *you* into his world every day. He might not have asked you to be his girlfriend yet, but you're who he wants, Riley. Besides, Shelby has her eyes set on Luke."

Riley eyed me warily. "How are you so certain?"

"Well, for one, I'm an outsider watching it unfold. It is much clearer to someone outside looking in. She blushes when Luke is mentioned, and her whole demeanor softens. I think she appreciates Randy's trust and support, but no more than someone would appreciate brotherly or sisterly support. It's not like that with them."

She sniffed. "Ugh, I feel so stupid. I should know that. I mean, we hang out together and spend time. He's always so kind and considerate to me; why would I doubt that?"

"It's normal, Riley. You care for him a lot, which means the thought of losing what you have, even if you want more, is scary. It feels out of your control. It's okay to be worried about losing what you have. It makes you respect it more. Cherish it."

"Thank you. I mean it."

I grinned. "Any-time."

She nudged my shoulder. "You know, you could have someone like that too."

I rolled my eyes. "Let's not go there."

She huffed. "Why not? You reserve yourself. Your wall is massive. If you removed it a little, what could it hurt?"

"Plenty. And I don't need love or like or lust. I'm perfectly happy with how my life is."

"Oh really? How was this weekend then?"

I put distance between us as I pretended to struggle with a different box. "It was fine."

"Liar. You've been closed off about what happened. You've barely spoken about how your mom reacted or how things are going with Drew. Shelby saw the two of you together at the theater. It appeared to be going better than you've stated."

"We get along; that isn't a newsworthy topic."

She crossed her arms and stood between the box and me. "Sophie, this is what I mean. You have such insight into my life and Shelby, but you completely avoid any chance that someone could care for you. I'm honestly surprised you let us in."

"What? I'm not that reserved. I'm just picky."

"It's more than picky, Sophie. I worry that you're so closed off you'll miss a chance with someone who is worth it."

"If they're that worth it, then it will work. If it doesn't, then it wasn't worth it."

She shook her head. "That's so stubborn, Sophie. So many people care about you, and more would too if they knew who you are. You can't stay guarded for forever."

I harrumphed. I wasn't that closed off. I made friends easily. I spent time with my family. So what if I wasn't drooling over a boy and making myself crazy wondering if he liked me? There was nothing wrong with that. There was also nothing wrong with being a little skeptical of people and their motives. I was being safe, that was all.

~

Three hours later and we had successfully emptied all the boxes, had stacked them in separate rooms, and had completed the forty baskets.

I leaned against the wall as I sat on the floor. "Wow. Well yay for being done that."

Shelby giggled. "Yeah, now to finish up the decorations and all for the festival."

My face paled. "What? Decorations too? I didn't sign up for those."

"Relax, Sophie. A company is handling the decorations, but I gotta go tomorrow to make sure it is set up and perfect for Saturday. You're still working a booth Saturday morning, right?"

"Of course."

Shelby twisted leftover ribbon around her finger. "I just wanted to make sure. Wasn't sure with …"

I knew what she was referring to. I also understood why she didn't fully explain, but it made the whole night feel dirty and gross—like I had murdered someone, instead of just getting drunk at a party.

"Mama insisted that a promise made is a promise kept. I couldn't get out of it if I wanted to."

"Good, because I really need you."

"I'll be there. I just hope not for the whole day."

"Nope. I have you scheduled from eight to eleven. Then the rest of the day is yours."

"Perfect. I can work and then be locked away."

Everyone's eyes widened.

"Relax. I'm not on house arrest. It was a joke."

"Ha-ha," Riley said.

I sighed. "I'm so ready for Easter break."

Randy nodded. "Absolutely. I need that whole week to recover from the spring festival."

Riley rubbed the inside of Randy's thumb. "You need to slow down."

"I'll slow down when it's over. Besides, Shelby is the one with the crazy schedule. She's running faster than I am with this."

Shelby shrugged. "Rowes have to do what they must to pull off a party."

I rolled my eyes. "Another Vivian motto?"

Shelby giggled. "How'd you guess?"

"It's all snobby."

"That it is."

I checked the time on my phone. "Well, we have school tomorrow, and Mama just might put me on house arrest if I don't get home. Can I bum a ride?"

Riley stretched and stood. "I'll take you home. I need to head home anyway. It's getting late, and I have a few more things to do for school tomorrow." She stared between Shelby and Randy who still sat on the floor. "You two going to manage without us?"

They nodded.

"I don't have a long commute," Shelby said.

"I'll be leaving too. We need to go over a few more details on the checklist," Randy said.

Riley nodded and scooted close to Randy, dropping her voice. "Text me when you get home?"

He nodded and wrapped his arms around her.

She melted into his embrace and shut her eyes.

The hug wasn't long but was so tender between the two of them.

I turned to give them privacy and checked my messages. Surprisingly, Mama hadn't texted or called yet. "I'll wait by your car, Riley."

I stepped from the room and back down the hallway. They deserved a few minutes of privacy, and I needed some air.

The sky was clear as the stars twinkled. The air was warm with a light breeze. Spring was definitely in Honey Cove, and I was certainly for it.

The door creaked.

My eyes widened as I spotted Shelby. "I didn't expect it to be you."

Shelby shrugged and stood next to me, peering skyward. "They looked like they needed a minute."

"You picked up on that too, huh?"

She nodded. "I know it's difficult with how much time he's spending on the project. I don't want to get in the way of that."

"She's just frazzled at the moment."

Shelby's eyebrow rose.

"I think she's getting overwhelmed with how she feels and how things are going. She's at the moment where losing what she has would be painful. They'll be fine. They just need to define things or redefine them in my opinion."

"I can understand that."

"Things okay with you?"

Shelby shifted her weight. "Yes. I just wish I knew for sure that this whole project would go well. I so badly want to prove the jerks on the board wrong about us. They just act so smug, especially Mr. Tate. I swear ever since I told Tabitha and Priscilla to take a hike, he has made it his mission to be awful to me every time."

"I can't imagine having all that pressure. And he's an idiot. What grown man takes out a vendetta on a teenage girl?"

Shelby snorted. "You'd be surprised." She sighed and kicked a rock. "They aren't all bad. Most of the men are decent; they're just so stuck in their ways. It's so frustrating."

"How's your parents with it all?"

"Mother is silent. She doesn't generally ask about the progress. Father seems to be content with the situation. I'm just waiting for another condition to pop up or for Mother to come up with a reason to control my life again."

"Well, I think you're doing great and if they can't see that, they're crazy. Even though I don't like the man for my mama, Rowan has said you seem to be rocking it. So not everyone thinks you'll fail."

Shelby squeezed my arm. "Thanks."

Riley exited the guesthouse and looked between us both.

"You okay?" I asked.

She nodded. "Ready to go?"

"Yep." I turned to Shelby and waved. "See you tomorrow at school."

Shelby waved and walked back inside.

We climbed into her car in silence and eased from the driveway. Music filled the ride to my house. I didn't ask her about her talk with Randy, and she didn't ask me about what she interrupted.

CHAPTER 15

The Saturday morning sun was brilliant; the sky was blue with very few clouds. The weather was supposed to get close to seventy-five degrees today, and I was so ready to absorb the warmth and vitamin D.

Mama shuffled around the booth, arranging and rearranging pamphlets, products, and the decorations.

"Mama, it's good. Shelby already approved of the setup. It's fine. Stop worrying."

Mama sneered at me. "It's my employer, and I want to show them what I can do."

I relaxed my hand over hers. "It's good and they know that."

She nodded. "Okay. Do you understand everything in this booth? You're the first person they'll see, so I want to make sure you're set."

"I'm good, Mama. Shelby already coaxed me through my duties, purpose, and what to do in certain situations. I have her number pulled up in my phone, and she set me to a certain tone if I need her. I'm good. It's only three hours."

Mama smoothed her shirt overtop her jeans. "Okay. I'll go

check on the other booth for Rowe Industries on the opposite side. Rowan is setting that one up to focus on the bigger opportunities in combining forces with Rowe Industries. We'll be by around eleven to relieve you, then I thought we could spend some time together, all of us."

My stomach dropped. I knew that ultimately her goal was for us to spend more time, but it didn't matter how many times I did, the mention of Rowan around always unnerved me.

I nodded and waved her away with my hands. "The festival is opening any minute, and I don't want you hovering around the booth. It might scare off people."

"Okay, okay. I'm going. Let me know if you need anything."

My shoulders untensed when she walked away. Having her around added extra pressure to me. I didn't want to be under a microscope for my entire shift. I could handle distributing pamphlets and discussing the products Rowe Industries offered. We had free samples, so it wasn't like I was selling any merchandise. This was baby stuff.

I double checked my area and where the replacements were under the table. If the crowd slammed us, I wanted to know where everything was so I could restock it in as little a time as possible.

I crouched under the table.

Someone coughed on the other side.

I jolted and banged my head on the underside of the table. "Ow," I said as I rubbed my head.

"Oh, I'm so sorry."

The familiar voice startled me. "Drew? What are you doing here? It's crazy early."

He nodded. "I'm here today to see what I can do at the theater's booth and then see what I can get into."

I laughed. "Get into? *You* get into something?"

He shrugged. "You never know about me."

My eyebrow rose. "You say that like you get in trouble or do sinister things."

"I don't know about sinister, but who says I'm a goodie two shoes?"

"I guess no one."

He adjusted his glasses farther up on his nose. "Well, I'll let you get back to it. I didn't mean to startle you. Maybe I'll see you later?"

I nodded. "Good luck at the booth."

He waved and turned to walk. "You too."

I watched until he was out of sight and crawled under the table to fish out more products. The doors would open any minute, and it was always wise to be prepared.

~

"Wow," Shelby remarked. "The samples are all gone. I had prepped out enough for what I thought would last all day."

I shrugged. "People were keen on the products, and when they found out they were free, the line stretched on. It was a struggle to keep up, but I think we did alright."

"I'd say." Shelby eyed the clipboard where people could sign up to join the Rowe Industries newsletter to stay up to date on products and new releases. "There are almost a hundred names on this list."

"What can I say? I'm a charmer."

Shelby giggled. "Well, I'll take it today. Are you sure you don't want to stick around longer?"

"I'm positive. I've loved helping at the booth, but standing here is killing my legs. It's worse than being at the ticket podium."

Shelby nodded. "Well, I release you oh-so-charming Sophie."

I rolled my eyes. "Don't be so dramatic."

Shelby nudged my arm. "What are you going to do now?"

"I get to hang out with my family. Hopefully, we can all chill later?"

"Maybe, depends on if anything comes up. But text me when your mom releases you. I'll see what I'm up to." Shelby checked her phone. "Have you seen Riley yet?"

"Nope. I figured she would be here by now." I shrugged. "Who knows, but I know she wouldn't miss it. She wants to support Randy as best as she can."

Mama, Caleb, and Rowan strolled toward the booth. Mama and Rowan held hands as Caleb appeared to be nonstop talking.

Great, just what I need.

Rowan nodded to Shelby. "Hello. Fabulous festival, Shelby. Your father will be so proud."

Shelby beamed. "Thank you. I should get back to checking on the vendors. Sophie is free to go mingle."

Mama smiled. "Bye, Shelby." She turned to me. "Ready?"

I inhaled deeply and nodded. They turned and walked from the booths and more toward the center of Honey Cove Park featuring little amusement rides—nothing fancy, mostly for the little kids—a Ferris wheel, and the spring-themed version of a hayride.

I stared at the tractors pulling the wagons. Flowers dripped from their every surface, while different colored flower petals filled the tractor bed.

Mama stopped and stared. "Wanna take a ride?"

I sighed, only too aware this was inevitable. Mama loved hayrides, so why wouldn't she want to do a spring-themed one?

We all nodded and hopped onto the step at the back of

the wagon. I got on first, walked as far back as there was space then sat.

Mama sat next to me, followed by Rowan then Caleb.

The wagon lurched forward, knocking me into the boy next to me. "I'm so sorry," I said as I regained my posture from the sudden movement. "I'm not usually clumsy; they just caught me off guard."

The boy turned to face me, and my jaw slackened.

Drew chuckled. "Well, what a surprise. Fancy bumping into you here."

My eyes widened. "I guess we're destined to run into each other at every turn."

Drew's right eyebrow arched. "Destined, huh? Funny, I didn't picture you as someone who believed in destiny."

"I-I don't. That's just an expression."

"Relax. I'm just messing with you."

"I know."

Drew looked around me to Mama. "How are the Grahams doing today?"

"We're fine."

At the mention of our last name, Mama turned. "Drew! How nice to see you. How are you?"

Drew smiled and proffered his hand over me. "I'm good, Mrs. Graham. It's nice to see you."

Mama blushed. "Please call me Faye. You know me well enough to call me by my first name. Mrs. Graham makes me feel old."

"Faye it is."

Mama looked around Drew. "Taking a ride by yourself?"

Drew nodded. "I figured it was a beautiful day, might as well."

Mama smiled. "That is so true. Always can enjoy a wagon ride." Mama's eyes sparkled. "And you know, you could keep

Sophie company. It has been so long since I've seen you two spend time together. Might even be nice."

My eyebrows drew together, and I tried to subtly shake my head.

"Oh, I wouldn't want to intrude," Drew said. "Besides, she sees my face enough at the theater. Wouldn't want to crowd her."

"Nonsense. Sophie doesn't think that, do you, Soph?"

I shook my head as I pinched the inside of my hand. "Of course not. I don't mind at all."

"See? It's perfect. Besides, I couldn't possibly look at your mother in the eyes at the next neighborhood gathering if I let you sit by yourself on this gorgeous day."

Drew smiled. "That's very thoughtful of you. Thank you."

She nodded and nudged my elbow.

Clearly, Mama thought she was being subtle.

I faced Drew, who sat with his arms to his sides and his head tilted to one side. "I'm sorry about her. She … well, I have no idea."

Drew chuckled. "It's fine, Sophie. We're good now, or at least I think we are?"

"Yeah. I mean, I think so too."

"I'm glad. It's nice to be able to be around you again." He leaned into my arm then shifted back. "I've missed our friendship, you know."

I smiled. "Me too."

I did miss the friendship. It was easier before feelings were involved. I didn't have to worry about what happened. Plus, of course, that was before my dad died.

The wagon lurched forward as we started around the path. "Do you remember that one time at Jenna's where we had the whole trampoline soaked in the summer?"

Drew's brows knitted and suddenly dropped. "You mean when Jenna got the idea to add soap?"

I giggled. "Yes! We were covered in soap suds in seconds."

Drew chuckled. "It was a mess, and, if I recall, we all got in so much trouble."

"Mm-hmm. She always got us in trouble."

"That she did."

Tables and people blurred past as we rode along. "Have you had a chance to explore?"

"Yep. A little bit of time."

"Anything good?"

"Lots of neat booths. There are local craft makers who have set out their things. Cool handmade bracelets and such."

"Yeah? I haven't seen those yet."

"Well, if you have time, I can show you … if you want. I know you used to like the braided cord bracelets."

"You remember that?"

"Of course. That one summer, you had your whole arm covered. It was almost to your elbow."

"What? Nuh-uh."

He nodded. "Yes, it was. Like two inches were free of bracelets."

I laughed. "I haven't thought about that summer in such a long time." It was the last summer my dad had been alive. We didn't know it at the time that there would never be another barbeque for Fourth of July. Or that we wouldn't make it to Christmas together.

I shook my head, hoping the thoughts would go with it.

"You miss him, don't you?"

My head snapped to face Drew. "How'd you know that's what I was thinking about?"

"It might have been a while since we've hung out of our own accord, but I'll never forget the face you make when you think about him. Your face shifts, and your eyes become so sad its unbearable to watch. Even now, the pain is so sharp in your eyes."

"Oh."

Drew reached toward my bare knee but retreated. "It's okay to still miss him. I can't imagine that kind of loss ever heals completely."

I rubbed my left eye. "I know. I just don't like to dwell on it. It doesn't change anything."

Drew nodded. "There's also the Ferris wheel and amusement park rides."

"Now those I saw."

I was thankful the conversation shifted. Drew didn't push, which was a blessed change compared to others in my life.

"Yeah? Would you go on any?"

"No. They looked like baby rides."

"Psh. I don't think so. Did you see how high the Ferris wheel is?"

"That's barely off the ground."

"Oh yeah? Well, I dare you to go on it then. Prove that it really is a baby ride."

I proffered my hand. "Deal."

He shook it, and my hand suddenly felt clammy. Why the heck did it do that? I let go and wiped my hand on my shorts.

The wagon stopped moving, and I looked around. We were already back at the starting point. "The ride is over already?"

"Yep," Drew said.

I had missed the entire ride. It had felt like thirty seconds. Had I really been enjoying my talk with Drew so much that I hadn't noticed us complete the entire trip? I shook my head; that couldn't have been it. It must have been a quick ride. That was all.

Mama clapped then stood.

Drew outstretched his hand to help me up.

I took it. He lifted gently, and I was on my feet. "Thanks."

He nodded.

I followed Mama off the wagon.

"That was a wonderful ride; you could just see all of Shelby's and Randy's hard work on this festival." Mama stretched and winked at me. "Everyone ready for some food?"

"Always," Caleb answered.

Mama laughed. "I know you're hungry, Caleb. That's a never-ending pit you have."

"I could eat," Rowan said.

I nodded.

Drew stepped down from the wagon.

"Drew, you want to join us?"

My face paled as I turned to face Drew.

Drew's eyes widened. "I don't want to intrude any more than I already have. You all should spend the time together."

"You two looked like you were getting along so well on the wagon ride. Why don't you come? No one here minds," Mama said.

Drew gazed at me. "What do you think, Sophie?"

I shrugged. "Sure, if you want to join us."

"Then it's settled," Mama said.

I resisted the urge to sigh. I couldn't tell if Mama was pushing us together or if she wanted me in a good mood to be around Rowan and she thought Drew could manage that. I was technically still in trouble from my last weekend. It made no sense, but whatever it was, I just hoped everyone avoided embarrassing me. If Caleb or anyone else divulged any embarrassing stories, I would severely make them pay.

We followed the crowd toward the vendors serving food.

"We have a few options. It looks like Over Easy's has a booth with some of their menu items, or we could try a different booth. Or we could go to Over Easy's and eat inside. What do ya'll think?"

"It might be nice to relax in a booth at Over Easy's," Rowan said.

Caleb nodded.

"Sophie and Drew? What do you think?"

"I'm fine with whatever, Mrs. … I mean Faye."

"Same," I said.

"Okay, then let's walk to Over Easy's. Who knows, maybe there'll be no lines since everyone is eating here."

Mama and Rowan held hands and linked together as we walked.

The act made me shiver. Coupled with the look Drew was giving me, I couldn't tell what I should be feeling.

Mama was right. Most people were focused in the park with the festival. Barely anyone was inside Over Easy's.

A hostess ushered us to a table near the front with six chairs. Mama sat at the end of the table, with Caleb across from her and Rowan next to him. I sat next to Mama with Drew next to me.

A waiter named Roger appeared at the table to take our orders. "Good afternoon. What can I start you off with?"

We gave our drink orders and stared at the menu as Roger got them ready.

Drew nudged my elbow. "What are you going to get?"

I shrugged. "Not sure yet. I don't usually have lunch here. Maybe a salad?"

Drew eyed me warily. "A salad? Really? Since when do you eat all the leafy greens?"

I rolled my eyes. "I eat healthy when I want to. It doesn't have to be a big deal."

Drew chuckled. "I just remember you being a burger girl."

"Things can change."

"Maybe."

Hmmph. What did he think he knew? I could change my order

and it not be a big deal. "Well, Mr. Burger Boy, what are you getting?"

"I didn't say I was about burgers. I just saw you as someone who was."

"Mm-hmm. You didn't answer yet."

"I might get their chicken pot pie."

"Now that sounds appealing."

Drew smirked.

"So, Drew. Where've you been lately?" Caleb asked.

I cringed. "Caleb, why don't you focus on your menu. Use it to practice your reading abilities."

Caleb stuck out his tongue. "I'll do as I please. I merely asked a question to our guest."

Mama patted Caleb's hand. "That's very nice, Caleb. But we don't ask nosy questions like that."

Drew cleared his throat. "I don't mind. I've been around. I work at the theater now."

Caleb's jaw slackened. "With her? Dude, bad move."

Rowan chuckled. "Why don't we let Sophie and Drew catch up while you tell me about your golf practice."

I exhaled and turned away from Caleb. "Sorry, little brothers and all."

"No worries. He's just curious."

"Maybe, but he drives me crazy. It's infuriating."

"Well, that's why he does it."

"Oh yeah? Now you know little brothers?"

"Not necessarily, just an observation." He took a sip of his soda. "Just like I observed a tension you have around Rowan. Pretty intense."

He could tell how I felt about Rowan? Did that mean I was that obvious, or was he focusing on me? I wasn't sure which one I hoped it was.

Drew leaned closer as Roger took everyone's orders.

"Don't worry about being obvious. I don't think anyone is watching you to tell."

My eyes widened. Had I said something out loud? How could he read my mind so accurately? I wiggled in my chair. I didn't like people knowing what I thought, and what was worse, I wasn't sure how Drew would use that ability.

*L*unch turned out well. No one mentioned any embarrassing stories, and other than in the beginning, Caleb minded his own business, which was a miracle. I still couldn't figure out Drew. He had changed the subject to school and work, but I still didn't know how he had read me so clearly. It was unnerving.

We walked from Over Easy's toward the festival. It had gotten even busier since we had gone for lunch.

"Wow. I didn't think there were that many people in Honey Cove," I said.

Mama nodded. "It certainly has picked up. Sophie, can I talk to you for a second?"

My stomach lurched as Mama tilted her head to the side. "Sure."

Mama leaned toward Rowan. "We'll be right back."

I looked at Drew who busied himself with his phone. He either pretended to ignore our mini chat or really was oblivious to it.

When we had scooted to the side, Mama paused. "Why don't you and Drew wander around for a bit by yourselves? We can meet up in a few hours to head home."

My eyes widened. "I thought I was dead or grounded or both?"

Mama shrugged. "You are, but you've done a good job this

week. It's up to you, of course, but if you're interested, I give my blessing."

I rolled my eyes. "Your blessing? Is this a pushing thing?"

"No. I just meant you've earned a little freedom. You can be grounded again when we drive home."

"Okay. If you're sure."

Mama nodded and strolled to the group.

Drew stowed his phone in his pocket and smiled.

"Rowan, Caleb, let's check out the booths for a minute."

Caleb groaned. "I don't want to go to the Rowe booth."

Mama glared. "It's for a minute; you'll barely notice." She faced Drew. "It was so nice to see you, Drew. Tell your momma hello for me." She waved and shuffled Rowan and Caleb away from us.

I kicked my shoe against the grass. "I've been freed."

Drew cocked an eyebrow.

"I'm technically grounded, not to mention I was slated to spend forever with them."

Drew chuckled. "It wasn't that bad, but what shall you do with your new freedom?"

I shrugged. "Still up to tour the craft booths and for me to prove you wrong about the Ferris wheel?"

Drew peered over the top of his glasses. "Is that so? Well, lead on."

I took a step and then stopped.

"Did you lose your bravery?"

"No. I just ... which way is it?"

Drew pointed to the left. "This way, if you mean the booths."

I nodded and changed course. "So, you didn't really explain why you're here alone today. I understand the whole theater booth, but its Saturday. Why aren't you spending it out doing something?"

Drew shoved one hand in his pocket. "I didn't have any other plans."

My brows knitted. "Really? Well, what do you usually do for fun?"

"I read or listen to music."

"No, I mean with others."

"You're looking at it."

I gasped. "You do everything by yourself? Why?"

"I just do. I don't mind being alone."

I shivered. "That sounds like the worst way to spend a weekend. You should get out more."

"Is that an invitation? Because otherwise, I tend to travel alone. I haven't found my niche in high school. At this point, I doubt I ever will."

"But Courtney says you're so funny and carefree. How can that person not have friends?"

Drew raised an eyebrow. "Courtney said … Do you two discuss me?"

"I-I … We, no."

Drew chuckled. "Well, apparently you do."

"It was just the time I met her and also when I shadowed her. She was telling me she had never seen you so serious."

"Oh."

"It's fine. It was my fault, which I told her."

His eyes widened.

"No, not about that. I said it was my fault you were so serious. Our past had baggage, that's all. I didn't tell her what happened."

"It happened a long time ago. I wouldn't have cared if you did."

The booths spread around us. Drew led us down one aisle. Table after table was lined with handmade trinkets, jewelry, and bags.

"This is absolutely stunning. I had no idea there were so many crafters in this area with such fine products."

Drew nodded. "I knew you'd like it."

I stared into Drew's deep-brown eyes. "I really do." I studied each table, not wanting to miss anything.

Drew was patient, even though I knew my pace was imperceptible, as if a snail.

The third table down had the braided cords. "These are awesome."

Drew nodded, dangling one around his finger. The colors were dark blue, white, and turquoise; it was stunning.

"That combination is perfect. Riley would love those colors."

Drew picked up a purpley one adorned with different shades of purple, almost like a bruise as it healed.

I eyed it in his hand.

He brought it closer until he set it into my hand. "But those are your colors."

I nodded as I stared at it. I hadn't worn these bracelets in so long, but I missed them. It was like a piece of who I was and had lost was being delivered to me again. I checked the price for both and clutched them in my hand.

The lady who made them sat behind the table.

Before I could let her know I was ready, Drew grasped my hand. "Let me."

"What? No. I couldn't possibly."

"Your mom paid for my lunch, and you've been gracious enough to let me walk around with you today. I want to."

I nibbled the bottom of my lip. "Drew ... I don't deserve—"

He put his finger to my lip. "Do not say you don't deserve it. Think of it as an act of truce and us moving past our baggage."

I tried to focus on his words, but the pressure of his

finger on my lip sent feelings through my body I couldn't explain. I nodded, unable to form any coherent sentences to argue otherwise.

Drew handed the lady money in exchange for a bag with the bracelets. He passed the bag to me.

"Thank you. I really do appreciate it."

He nodded. "Shall we venture to the Ferris wheel?"

"Okay." I couldn't believe what had just happened. No one had ever bought something for me besides family, let alone Drew. Did he really mean for it to be a way to move forward?

The line to the Ferris wheel was shorter than I had expected. We only waited a few minutes before it was our turn to sit.

The Ferris wheel attendant locked the bar across into the mechanism then moved to the others.

I gripped the bar.

"You're not nervous, are you?" Drew asked.

"Of course not. It's important to hold on."

He chuckled. "If you say so."

I heard the whirr of the wheel then felt the motion. We went around a few times in silence. I looked out as far as I could see to view Honey Cove. The view was breathtaking. In the distance, I could see the glimmer from the cove and the land that seemed to stretch forever.

When we neared the top, we slowed until it finally stopped.

"Still think it's a baby height?"

"Maybe not, but it's not anything scary like some of the world-famous Ferris wheels."

"I'll certainly give you that." Drew faced me the best he could in the seat. "I've had a really nice day today."

I smiled. "Me too."

"I didn't expect to hang out with the Grahams. It's been a throwback."

I giggled. "I suppose it has—hopefully, a good one."

"Yes, although Caleb is nothing like I remember."

I snorted. "He has grown into himself, that is for sure. He drives me bonkers. I can't wait for him to start freshmen year and be pounded down a few pegs."

"That's a little harsh, don't you think?"

"Nope. He is insufferable this year. Must be an eighth-grade boy thing."

"Possibly. But nothing wrong with being confident."

"No, but there is a point when it crosses into arrogance."

"Ah yes, well, he'll learn, or he won't. But high school can be cruel. I hope, for his sake, he doesn't experience that."

"Okay, well, now I feel like a jerk."

Drew chuckled. "Not my intention. I get your perspective too, but he just loves his sister. He seems very proud of you."

I stared at him warily. "Have you, like, intercepted phone calls and bugged my house? You got all that just from today?"

He nodded. "When you aren't the center of the topic, you notice a lot about people. I've had practice at people watching."

The Ferris wheel whirred to life again. I considered Drew's statement. Was he lonely if he was always watching others? Or was it just a habit he had developed over time?

I studied his features as he looked out past the festival. The frames of his glasses looked a little crooked, and his hair was longer than I remember him having as kids. I smelled a subtle remnant of cologne and saw slight stubble on his chin. He wasn't the same seventh grader Jenna and I had tortured. He was grown and wiser. That fact made me feel the guilt I had grown accustomed to. I hoped I hadn't been the cause of his changes. Had I set him on a path to be alone? Had I ruined his ability to trust friends?

We stopped, and the attendant unlocked the bar. We climbed out and stood to the side.

I fiddled with the bag carrying my bracelets. "See you tomorrow?"

He nodded. "You want me to help you find your mom?"

"That's okay. We preplanned a location. I'll wait there until they arrive." I checked the time on my phone. "Honestly, by the time I walk back there, they'll probably be there too."

"Okay. Well, see you tomorrow."

I watched him walk away. He turned back once, waved then continued into the festival, weaving around other people. When I had prepared to work at the festival, I had never expected the day would have turned out like this.

Our meeting spot was at the Rowe booth where I had started the morning. While I waited, I grabbed the purple bracelet from the bag. I pushed it over my hand and onto my wrist. It fit perfectly there.

I smiled as I saw Mama approaching me. It was time to go, but that was okay. She had allowed me out of my consequences for longer than I had expected.

Mama stopped in front and smiled. "Ready to go?"

I nodded and followed her out. Maybe things weren't as bad as I thought they were.

CHAPTER 16

I stared at the first *F* I had ever received in my schooling career. My physics teacher chose today to hand back our tests, and as the paper floated into my hands, I was overwhelmed with disbelief. I tried to recall when we had taken this test, let alone if I had studied. I came up short on both accounts. I gripped the test tightly. This would tank my grade. What was I going to do?

I walked by Mrs. Willow's desk and stopped. "Mrs. Willow?"

She peered from her papers. "Yes, Sophie?"

I twisted the test between my hands. "Is it possible I could have extra credit or something to bring up this grade?"

She folded her hands. "Ah, yes. I must admit I was surprised to find your name on the front page after calculating the score. You're usually setting the curve."

"I-I know. That's why I was hoping there was a chance?"

"Sophie, you know I don't give out extra credit. There are more tests before the end of the year. I suggest you do the best you can on each of them. Your previous grades have cushioned this test, but more down this path and I'm afraid you would certainly impact your GPA."

I nodded. "Okay. Thank you, Mrs. Willow."

"Have a good evening."

I trudged from her room to my locker. I can't believe I failed a physics exam. I never failed anything. I leaned my head on my locker door. This wasn't how everything was supposed to happen. Why couldn't surprises stop happening at this point? It was too much.

Sneakers shuffled to my side then stopped. When the sneakers didn't disappear, I looked to see who was wearing them.

Drew's eyes were laced with concern. "You okay?"

I shook my head.

"What's wrong?"

I showed him the test and stared at the contents of my locker.

"Ouch. What about the rest of your grade? If it's just one test, it won't impact it that much."

I glared at him. "It will, considering how poorly I failed and that I had straight *A*s going. This must've brought me down to at least a *C*."

Drew crossed his arms. "Did you ask for extra credit?"

I nodded. "Mrs. Willow doesn't do that, which I knew, but I had hoped she would make an exception."

"So, what will you do?"

I shrugged. "Study like crazy, I guess." I sighed. "This was supposed to be a good trimester. I need it for colleges when I send them my application."

"I'm sure they can overlook one class, and you haven't failed out yet, so don't panic."

I half smiled. "Yeah, right."

Drew shifted his backpack from one shoulder to the other. "Listen, why don't you let me drive you home?"

My eyebrows rose. "I can walk. I like the exercise."

"I know you can, but I don't want to leave you like this."

I closed my locker. "You aren't going to take no for an answer, are you?"

He shook his head.

"Fine." I started to walk but stopped. "Wait. Why did you come over here in the first place?"

Drew chuckled. "I always walk by your hallway on the way from school. My last class isn't far from here. I saw you leaning quite pathetically against the locker. I couldn't exactly ignore that."

"Ah. Gotcha."

We walked in silence from the school toward his car. I heard the doors unlock, and I climbed into the front seat.

He adjusted the radio's volume then pulled from the school parking lot. "So, what's the real issue?"

"What do you mean?"

"You don't just get an *F* on a test, Sophie—at least you didn't used to—so unless I missed a massive memo about character change, something else is going on."

I crossed my arms. "How do you do that? It's frustrating, you know. Sometimes people want to sulk in their own crap."

Drew raised his eyebrow then faced the road. "Is that what you really want, or are you mad someone called you out on things?"

"I don't know. I'm annoyed that you barely have interacted with me in years, and now it's like a mirror reflects off me and tells you everything I'm thinking. I don't understand how the heck you manage to do that."

"Okay, fair enough. I like to think I still know you, Sophie. I was around when your dad died, and I think you've gotten away with isolating people who knew you before and who could call you out when you're avoiding your feelings. I saw how you were around Rowan. It was like someone sucked out everything that made you who you are when he enters your perimeter." He stole a glance. "Is he a bad guy?"

I wiggled farther down in the seat. "Yes." I sighed. "No. Okay? No, he isn't a bad guy."

"Then—"

I shook my head. "No. Why does it have to be something else. You said it yourself; you used to know me well. Things change in almost six years. I mean, you did—either that or I didn't know who you really were. I can change too. Why can't I just focus on the fact I failed a physics test and I need to pull up the grade?"

"You can focus on whatever you want, Sophie. I'm not trying to push you. If that's what you want to focus on, go for it." He paused and eyed me warily. "I just think you're avoiding the bigger picture."

I groaned. "Well, thanks, Mr. Therapist, but I'm good."

Our neighborhood pulled into view, then we traveled the short drive to his driveway. He put the car in Park, and I practically leaped from it.

"Thanks for the ride!" I shouted and ran to my house.

This was nuts. He was delusional. Nothing else was going on. Rowan had nothing to do with my classes, and I was allowed to not like him, even if he was a good guy. He could be a great guy, in fact, but it didn't make him right for Mama.

"Soph! Catch!" Courtney shouted as she tossed me several packets of popcorn kernels. The packets landed a foot in front of me.

Drew shook his head. "You could have knocked her out, Courtney. She's not a catcher; she's a runner."

Courtney giggled. "My mistake."

I eyed her warily. "Psh. You did that on purpose."

She winked and sauntered from the snack counter.

"She's in an ornery mood tonight."

I shrugged. "It is what it is. Will keep it interesting." My hand rested on my hip. "And I can catch things; I'm not inept with the upper half of my body."

"I didn't mean you were inept. I merely meant you focus on running."

"Maybe."

Drew leaned against the counter as I surveyed the lobby. Not many people had arrived to watch a movie on a Wednesday night. The upside was I didn't have to panic about not having enough snacks. The downside was it left plenty of time for Drew and me to talk ... which, after

Monday and my runaway act, I had no idea how that would go.

Drew adjusted his glasses. "Yanno, while Courtney is away, I wanted to let you know you're doing well with your probationary period."

My eyebrow jerked up. "I am?"

Drew nodded. "You listen to the customers, you complete your tasks, and you think about what else you could do instead of waiting to be told. Those are all great qualities."

My cheeks flamed. "Thanks. I just don't want to let anyone down."

"I think you're on a good path with Mr. Martin. If you keep performing like this, I think you have a good chance of being permanent."

Satisfaction oozed from my smile. "That's the goal."

Drew smiled and watched me. It wasn't his typical smiles I had been used to seeing lately. It was a genuine smile, one that made warmth spread through my body from my head to my toes.

He leaned closer. "I can't stop thinking about what you said on Monday."

The warmth faded as dread invaded.

"You mentioned people changing in five years, and you were right. I should've known better that we both wouldn't be the same as we were in seventh grade. Everyone grows."

The more he talked, the less I understood. Where was he going with this?

Drew turned his head from side to side as he gazed at the lobby. "No one is really here. I'm curious to see what's changed with us both."

My eyebrows knitted together. "How do you suggest we do that?"

Drew shrugged. "I don't know. For lack of a better name, twenty questions?"

I giggled. "You want to play twenty questions, but about our life?"

"Why not?"

"Okay. Who asks first?"

"You can if you want."

I cocked my eyebrow. "Deal."

"Favorite book."

"Easy. *Percy Jackson* series."

"Really? Still."

Drew nodded. "Can't beat an adventure novel mixed with mythology. You?"

"I don't know. I haven't read much in a while."

"Fair enough." He stroked his chin. "Hmm. Well, we know your favorite color is still purple. What do you watch the most of on TV now?"

"HGTV. You?"

"Not really watching live TV. I stream things, but that's about it."

"Still avoiding sports?"

Drew chuckled. "Pretty much. We all know you still live and breathe track." He shifted his weight off the counter as an elderly couple approached the counter. "Good evening, ma'am."

The lady smiled. "Hello, young sir. I would like two pretzels and cheese."

"Coming right up."

The lady turned toward me. "Two large popcorns as well please."

I nodded and shifted behind the machine.

The elderly man passed us to the soda machine and filled two large sodas.

"Any toppings?"

The lady shook her head.

"Here you go. Have a great time."

She strolled toward Drew as he finished placing the pretzels in their small containers.

How would these two people carry all this? It wasn't possible.

I scooted around the counter and walked toward her. "Ma'am, can I assist you to your theater?" I stared at Drew to make sure he wouldn't mind.

He nodded.

"Oh, you don't have to do that," she said.

"I don't mind at all. We aren't that busy, and I'd like to help you."

The older man smiled as he approached his wife.

"Well, Herbert, this young lady offered to help us." She grinned at Drew. "Such nice people working here."

I carried their popcorn as they grabbed their pretzels and drink and followed them to their theater room.

Courtney eyed me warily as I walked with them but said nothing.

When I returned, Drew had this glint in his eye I couldn't explain. I tucked a strand of hair behind my ear. "What?"

"That was very nice of you."

I shrugged. "They couldn't carry all of that themselves. I figured it was the least I could do."

"Very true. But also thoughtful in a way people don't always practice."

My cheeks heated as I considered his response. He was happy for me? No … it was different than that. I couldn't put my finger on it, but it unnerved my stomach.

Drew continued his questions, but all I could do was think about his reaction.

∾

My feet ached from standing still by the time my shift was over. Our conversation shifted in so many directions playing Drew's game, but I realized that I had been both right and wrong. He was familiar but, at the same time, had nuances I didn't know from before. It was nice to be around him again. It had an ease and understanding I hadn't gotten from Riley and Shelby, as if I could be who I was now while also being connected to who I was before.

Mama pulled up to the curb where I waited.

I hopped in and was grateful for the radio being loud. It meant no interrogations or questions—in other words, the best kind of ride with a parent. Unfortunately, it didn't last. Once the song had ended, Mama turned down the volume. "How was work?"

I shrugged. "Fine. You?"

"It was good. Things are good at work. I'm up for a promotion. Did I tell you that?"

I leaned toward her. "No. Is it a job you want?"

"Yep. Better pay and hours. I wouldn't have to work so many night shifts. I could be home in the evenings more for you and Caleb."

"Oh. Well, when do you find out?"

Was it bad that I selfishly didn't want her to get it? I had become accustomed to having freedom after school and in the evening. If she was home more, I could no longer do more of the things I wanted to.

"In a few weeks. I applied last week though. So, fingers crossed."

I pretended to hold my fingers crossed with as much enthusiasm as I could muster.

"So … did you work with Drew again?"

I rolled my eyes. "How subtle of you. Yes. All my shifts are pretty much with Drew. I have to shadow him."

"Oh, that's right. Well, how is it going?"

I sighed. "Do we always have to talk about work and Drew?"

"I'm just curious, is all. I have eyes, and you two seemed more in sync than I've seen in a while. I just wanted to check in."

"We had a good day … as friends and coworkers. That's it."

"Okay. Well, it's nice to see you around more people. You've blossomed so much this year. I'm just happy you have more people in your corner." Mama reached for my hand. "I worry about you."

I nodded. "Duly noted, but I'm fine." I cranked up the volume and hoped Mama would let it slide.

Thankfully, she took the hint and left the radio's volume alone until we got home. She grabbed her bag from the back seat, and I followed her as she unlocked the door.

"There's a package here," I said as I handed her the cardboard box.

Mama's eyes brightened. "Ooh! It's here."

"What's here?"

"At the festival, they had these portraits, and we took a few."

"Oh. Why didn't they just give them to you on Saturday?"

Mama ripped open the package and stared. "It took time to print."

I walked to the kitchen to grab a drink. Who went crazy over portraits? We had hundreds of photos together. Not to mention, why did she get pictures with Caleb and not me? I grabbed a water bottle and downed a few good gulps.

I turned the corner. "Mama? Wait—" I froze dead in my

spot. I blinked repeatedly, hoping my eyes weren't deceiving me.

Mama stood in the hallway, staring at the framed photo of her and Dad when they were younger. He had taken her dancing, and one of her friends had snapped the photo to commemorate it. I loved that photo. They both looked so happy together.

Mama slid the image from the back, set it on the floor and inserted the portrait from the festival in its place. Then she rehung it on the wall.

I tiptoed closer. The photo wasn't of her and Caleb but of her and Rowan.

Mama had replaced a photo with Dad for Rowan.

I nearly dropped the bottle and scooted past her. I shut my door and paced. What was she thinking? She couldn't replace a photo of Dad with *him*. He didn't belong on that wall. That wall was for family. It was for us. He wasn't part of us.

I sank to the floor, clutching my chest. How could she do this to us? To me? A sob escaped my mouth. I reached for a pillow off my bed and clutched it to my face. I screamed and cried until my head pounded. I couldn't believe it. I didn't want to believe it. What was next? Would she replace Caleb and me too? Would she have more kids and replace us like she just had to Dad?

I dragged my hand across my face, smearing the tears. How could she have loved him like she said and do that to his memory? This was his house. His family.

I grabbed my phone from the floor and scrolled. Tears dripped from my face onto the screen as they escaped without my permission. I found the group text and thumbed a message. *Easter break this weekend. Let's celebrate with a party. Who's in?*

Shelby replied first. *I don't know, Sophie. Luke comes home Friday.*

Me: *Perfect, bring him too. I know someone has to be having something.*

Riley's name appeared on the screen. *I'm out. Randy and I have an evening planned. Not to mention, Sophie, do you really want to go to another party so soon? Will your mom even let you?*

It's break. I've been good, she won't care. Shelby, please tell me you're in?

Shelby: *Fine. I'm in. I'll let you know what I find out.*

I scooted to my nightstand, still holding the pillow to my chest. I dabbed my eyes with the tissue and blew my nose. I slowly stood, changed into pajamas and collapsed into bed. Wave after wave hit me. My heart felt like it had broken into more pieces than when he had died. I would go to a party and forget.

The emptiness filled me, scratching at everything I had left.

It should have been Mama to die, not Dad. He would have never done this to her.

CHAPTER 18

"Are you sure this is a good idea?" Riley asked as she watched Shelby and I primp for the party.

"I think it's the perfect way to begin spring break. We've earned this."

"I'm just excited to see Luke tonight."

"While I'm super happy for you both, aren't we forgetting the last time?"

I rolled my eyes. "Don't you have to meet Randy soon?"

Shelby chuckled. "Sophie won't do that again, will you, Sophie?"

"No. Now stop worrying about it. You're killing my vibes."

Riley stared between us both. "I have such a bad feeling about this."

I raised an eyebrow. "Are you sure it's not the nervousness from seeing Randy? Isn't this a big evening for you both?"

"What? No. We're just spending time together. With everything, we haven't had time alone in a while."

I wiggled my eyebrows. "Ooh. Whatcha going to do with the alone time?"

Riley stole a pillow from Shelby's bed and chucked it at my head. "We're just spending time together. Stop getting it all twisted in your ridiculous ideas."

I held up my hands. "Okay. It was just a joke. Jeez."

Riley checked her phone. "I'm leaving. Please be careful. Text me when you two get back from the party."

Shelby nodded. "I promise. Now go have fun with Randy."

Riley smiled sheepishly and waved as she exited the room.

"You look hot, Sophie. It's a shame Drew isn't going with us."

I rolled my eyes. "I don't, and, whatever, we're friends."

Shelby giggled. "I know how that goes, and it's a far cry from where you two were before. Are you honestly going to tell me you don't feel anything for him?"

I crossed my arms and focused on my reflection. "I don't have any feelings for him."

Shelby nodded as if she still didn't believe me. "Mmkay. Well, I still mean it. Those capris and crop top look killer on you."

I twisted in the mirror, trying to see my outfit from behind. "You think so?"

"Yes."

I studied Shelby's longer skirt and flowy top that stopped a few inches before the top of the skirt, revealing a flat stomach. "Well, I certainly must up my game around you. No one will see me when you walk through the door. So, let me go first."

"Oh please. First of all, that's not true. Secondly, no one will do anything. I'm a Rowe; that deters boys right away. Third, Luke is meeting us outside, so I'd walk in with him.

Do you really think anyone would try to get my attention at that point?"

I shrugged. "Depends on the vibe between you and Luke."

Shelby inhaled sharply. "I'm so nervous. My stomach feels like it's on a rollercoaster. This is ridiculous. Why am I so worried?"

"It's been several months since you've seen him. I'm sure that has something to do with it."

"Maybe."

"Are we ready?"

Shelby nodded and grabbed her clutch from her bed.

"It's not at Brian's, is it?"

Shelby shook her head. "Nope. We'll be going to Asher Jacobs's house."

"Asher, as in, the captain of the baseball team?"

"Yep."

"How the heck do all these boys manage to have these awesome parties? Like, is that why they ascend into high school popularity, or is it a coincidence?"

Shelby giggled. "I have no idea. I don't analyze it. It's a party; you want to go or not?"

"Yes, fine. I just don't see how it's fair they can manage this social advantage and we're left without a chance."

"That's a tad dramatic."

"I disagree."

Shelby and I sat in her BMW. She adjusted her mirrors and fiddled with the radio until she found a pop station.

I had no idea which way Asher lived or how Shelby knew, so I was left to contemplate everything while I waited to get there. Mama had never said anything to me about the photo. I didn't know if she knew I had bawled my eyes out that night, but if she did, she didn't act on it. What was worse, Caleb hadn't even noticed it, and when Mama had pointed to the new photo, he had beamed.

Both were traitors. How could they possibly ignore the issue in what she had done? It had taken everything in me to keep myself together the last two days. I hadn't told anyone. I knew if they found out, they'd suspect my motives for the party.

Riley clearly already questioned why I wanted to go, but I couldn't have someone ruin it for me. I needed this. I felt so free that night. I would stop before I got sick and remain in that feel good rhythm. It wasn't a difficult concept to figure out.

I had always done what was right, been the good one. And what did it get me? My father had died, and Mama had replaced him faster than anything I had ever believed to be possible. I had earned time to relax and let go. If no one else understood that, it was their problem, not mine.

We pulled into a cul-de-sac that I was extremely familiar with. "Asher lives in my neighborhood?"

Shelby nodded and parked on the street at the end of the cul-de-sac. The house backed up to trees, and the neighbors were a fair distance away. Minus the obscene number of cars in this part of the neighborhood, you would have no idea it was a party.

Shelby locked her car and walked forward, then she suddenly stopped. "Oh my god."

I looked around, unable to figure out what had her freaked out. "What? What's wrong?"

Shelby held a hand to her stomach. "He's standing by the door."

"He? He who?"

I searched the front of the house until my gaze settled on Luke. "Luke?" I pushed her arm. "You had me freaked out because you saw Luke?"

"I'm sorry. I just haven't seen him in person in months. Wow, my stomach is flipping out."

I rolled my eyes. "Please do not be cutesy with each other in front of me. I see it with Randy and Riley, and if I have to add you two to it, I might vomit."

"Oh, whatever. If you don't like how we interact after months, you can walk around without us."

"Done deal."

The second Luke's gaze settled on Shelby, I could sense it. His shoulders relaxed, and his smile grew. I eyed Shelby, and she mirrored Luke's reaction.

Great, another lovesick duo to nauseate me with their feelings.

Luke waved at me. "Hey, Sophie." Then he froze as he reached for Shelby. Was he trying to hug her or shake her hand? He finally patted her shoulder, and I had to bite my lip to stifle a laugh. If they could barely greet each other, this would be a long night.

"I'm going to head in, Shelby. Find me when you're ready."

Shelby nodded as she stared at Luke.

They whispered to each other, but the words were drowned out as I entered the house, and the music and people carried away their conversation.

Asher's house was smaller than Brian's. The layout was less open and extravagant, yet somehow, there seemed to be more people in Asher's house than Brian had a few weeks ago. How was that possible?

I circled through the crowd, trying to find a place to sit or get a drink, but the mass number of bodies made it difficult. Finally, I broke through, and at the back of the house on the dining room table sat cups and drinks. I surveyed the choices and settled on a beer I didn't even read the brand name of. I opened the can, poured it into my cup then looked for a place to sit.

I could drink my beer, listen to the music, and people watch. I knew Shelby would eventually come in and see me with a beer, but by then, I'd hoped to already be on my second one. Then what would she do? She wasn't my mother, and I couldn't imagine her taking an overprotective approach the way Riley certainly would.

Maybe it was a good idea she hadn't come. She would have killed my buzz. I bobbed my head and swayed to the song playing over the speakers. It was an R&B hit from over a decade ago, but it still moved me.

Most of the people in the main area were dancing. Bodies next to bodies moved almost as one large entity. It was crazy to see.

I had been sipping my beer, until a familiar face lumbered toward me. I chugged it and sat the cup next to me, waiting for him to reach me. "Fancy seeing you here. I thought you stayed home and did the alone thing?"

Drew smirked. "Well, someone recently told me that I should get out more. I saw the party on the Buzz app and thought, why not? It isn't far from our houses."

"Interesting."

Drew's eyebrow rose as he spied my cup. "Why is that interesting?"

"I never thought you'd listen to me, much less venture out." My eyes widened. "Wait, did you seriously come to a party by yourself?"

He shrugged. "Maybe. What would it matter if I did?"

"Nothing. That's just incredibly sad."

"Oh?" He tried to dramatically look for people around me. "I don't see you with anyone."

"Shelby is outside with Luke. Well, maybe. That's the last place I saw her before I came in. I don't know if they're still out there or not."

"So, is Riley here too then?"

I shook my head. "No, she had other plans. We don't always go everywhere together."

Drew chuckled. "No one said you did. I merely noticed you three have become close. It's good you have someone there for you."

"Ha. That's the same thing Mama said to me." I crossed my arms. "Why does everyone think I *need* someone to be there for me? I make it just fine on my own."

"No one is doubting your independence, Sophie. But everyone needs someone. That's how humans work. You aren't exempt from that just because you think you are."

I crossed my arms and stood. I had underestimated the distance between Drew and me. Our bodies were close enough that our chests brushed, and the heat from his body reached me.

Between the first beer and the sudden closeness, I felt unsteady. I reached backward for the couch, when instead, I felt a hand grab mine.

"Woah. You okay?"

"I'm fine. I just need another drink."

He nodded. "Want me to get you one?"

"No. I can manage."

Drew stepped backward and gestured to the table.

I walked past him and headed to get a refill. I could feel his gaze on me as I refilled my cup with another beer. "I guess you have an opinion about me drinking something?"

"Nope. I didn't say anything." Drew shoved his hands in his pockets and stared at the floor.

I took a sip. "You don't have to say anything. I can feel your disapproval radiating from your body."

"Is that so?"

I hiccupped. "Yep. So, you might as well say it."

Drew shook his head. "I have nothing to say. Maybe you are misinterpreting this *disapproving energy.*"

"If it's not disapproval, what is it?"

Drew began to speak, but, a finger tapped my shoulder.

I turned and saw Shelby eyeing me as she stood next to Luke.

"Hey! You two made it in."

Shelby's cheeks blushed, but she remained focused on the cup in my hand. She smiled at Drew. "It's good to see you, Drew."

He nodded. "I should … uh. I should go meet my friends. It was good to see you all." He waved and pushed back through the crowd.

I frowned. He didn't explain what else his negative energy could have been, and I didn't think he had friends to actually meet. "This place is crazy. It's worse than Brian's."

Luke's eyes widened. "Did you turn into a party animal since I left?"

"No. This is the second party I've been to. Both were Sophie's ideas."

I raised my hand. "Guilty. I thought it would be fun."

Shelby turned to Luke. "Could you get us a couple sodas?"

Luke nodded and focused on the table as Shelby pulled me by the elbow a few feet from earshot. "What are you doing?" She poked me in the ribs. "You're drinking again?"

"Would you relax. It's just one beer. I won't overdue it like last time. That was an accident."

Shelby squeezed the bridge of her nose. "You ended up drunk last time because your body isn't used to alcohol. It won't take much for you to lose control. I thought last time scared you enough to be smarter next time?"

"Shelby, I'm fine. Seriously. I could run three miles right now. Go spend time with Luke. You don't need to babysit me."

Shelby crossed her arms. "Sophie, I don't know what your deal is lately, but please be careful. I'm here for you. I'd rather you be safe than end up like last time, regardless of who is here."

"I refuse to let you waste time with me when he's here. I saw how you both looked at each other. You need this time, so go take it. I won't go anywhere. I'll just sit on the couch in the other room and listen to the music. I'm fine. I promise."

Shelby twisted her clutch's band around her finger. I could tell she was considering it.

"Honestly, I won't move. You can watch me from afar if it makes you feel better. But I don't want to ruin the few days you have while he's home."

Luke shuffled to us, holding a cup in each hand. "Here you go, Shelby."

She smiled as she gazed at his face. "Thanks."

The dimple in Luke's cheek grew as he stared back at her.

"I'll be over here," I said as I scooted from them.

Luckily, Shelby listened and didn't follow me to an empty seat on the couch.

I surveyed the crowd, but Drew wasn't in here either. I frowned, wondering where he had disappeared to, if for no other reason than I was curious to hear what he was going to say.

The music shifted from an upbeat tempo to something slower. When the first chords played, my heart stopped. It was "Simple Man" by Shinedown. I was certain before the first lines blared over the speaker.

The buzz of the room stopped as the words soaked into me. A tear escaped down my cheek, and I swatted it away. How could this song play at this moment? I stared at the ceiling and willed the tears to disappear. I couldn't listen to this song right now. Who would put that on a playlist for a party anyway? The energy ran through me, as if I had stuck my finger into a socket and was being electrocuted.

It was in that minute I knew I would break my own rule. I couldn't sit here and deal with those feelings and not do something to numb them. I stared at the table with the beer and was relieved when Shelby was no longer standing there with Luke. I pushed through the crowd, grabbed two cans and searched for a place to be alone and drown out the song.

A small room off the main hallway provided the near silence. I sat in the corner and cracked open the beer. Then everything went fuzzy.

CHAPTER 19

The morning sun gleamed through the curtains. I blinked, trying to adjust my focus. The curtains were blue and definitely weren't what I had in my room. I tried to prop myself up but found that to be difficult. I stared at the bed and sheets I laid in. None of this was my stuff. *What in the world was going on?*

Then the pounding forced its way to the front of my mind. I winced as the throbbing in my head and the nausea suddenly took hold.

"Morning, sunshine," Shelby said.

I startled, nearly falling from the strange bed. "Jeez, Shelby. You scared me half to death." I leaned back, quickly regretting the fast movement as everything spun. I shut my eyes and willed things to stop spinning. I peeked open one eye and saw Shelby sitting on an armchair by the window.

"How ya feeling?" she asked as she blew over the top of something.

"Just peachy." I rubbed my eyes, hoping to remove myself from this stupor. "What happened? I don't remember getting here. In fact, where am I?"

Shelby sighed. "You're in the guesthouse. I brought you here after I found you passed out in the small room at Asher's."

"I passed out?"

"Apparently so. You were slouched against the wall, beer cans around you, with your head hung down. I'd say that would define passed out."

I slowly rubbed my hands down my face. "That sounds splendid. Ugh, I seriously remember none of that."

Shelby exhaled loudly.

"Are you okay?" I asked, staring at the ceiling.

"No, Sophie. I'm not. We made excuses the first time. We got you to your mom, and then last night, you practically promised us there would be no repeat. What has gotten into you? I'm not thrilled about having to babysit someone at a party. I can't even trust you by yourself."

"Can you not talk so loudly? It pierces my head."

Shelby growled. "I honestly don't care if it kills your brain cells at this point. You're acting ridiculous. Riley and I have talked, and we will *not* enable this behavior. We will not take you to anymore parties, and we certainly won't let you drink anything around us again."

"I-I know I screwed up."

"Sophie, it's more than that. You were passed out on that floor. God forbid if it had been someone other than Drew who found you."

I winced. "You sound like Mama."

"Well, I would think so. Sophie, I was terrified for you. Drew came and found Luke and me. He dragged us to that room and helped Luke carry you to my car. If he hadn't been at that party, I dread to think of what would have happened." Shelby sniffed. "I would have never forgiven myself if something horrible happened to you. I knew I shouldn't let you out of my sight. I was selfish and had agreed because I wanted to spend time with Luke. I should have known better."

"It's not your fault, Shelby. If anything had happened, it would be on me, not you."

"That's not how it feels. I drove you to that party. I left you alone. God, Sophie. I don't understand. This doesn't feel like you at all."

I sighed and tried to turn to my side. I moved inched by inch until I faced Shelby.

She rubbed the skin under her eyes as she looked to the ceiling. Was she crying?

"I'm sorry I scared you. Nothing happened, and I promise it won't happen in the future."

"Your damn straight it won't, because Riley and I won't go with you." She stood and stormed to the door. "Pull yourself together, Sophie." She opened the door and marched from the room, leaving me alone with everything.

I sighed and sunk into the bed. If I had felt stronger, I would have followed her. But alas, I could barely keep it together laying down, let alone trying to chase after someone who had just stormed from the room.

Her words added a new level of pounding to my head as they circled. She was right; I should have been more careful. Anyone could have found me and done anything; although I doubted Honey Cove was that kind of town, how did I know for sure? But what was worse was I could have done anything and not realized it.

I laid there as I forced myself to remember anything from last night. I remembered seeing Luke and Shelby and convincing her to leave me alone. I remembered Drew leaving when he had spotted them. I was pretty sure I had taken a cup to that couch and sat, but then what had happened?

Shelby cleared her throat and interrupted my thoughts. "I

brought you breakfast. Nothing crazy. Scrambled eggs, toast, and a sports drink. I figured anything more and you might throw it up."

I slowly propped myself up until I was sitting. "Thank you."

Shelby placed the tray in front of me and started to back up.

I placed my hand over hers. "Wait. I need to apologize. I scared you. I can't imagine if the roles had been reversed. I shouldn't have done that. I know I've not been like myself. I'm … I'm working on it."

Shelby sighed and sat at the edge of the bed. "I don't mean to berate you, Sophie. I know we all go through and have our things. I know you, of all three of us, talk about them the least. I don't know what's causing your pain, but I beg you to find a solution besides getting drunk at a party. Speaking for myself, I don't know if I can watch that spiral. As for Riley, well, I don't know. I can tell you that she's pretty terrified since last night." She patted my hand. "We're worried for you. We just want you to be okay, and if you need us, we're there." She peered into my gaze. "Okay?"

I nodded, then winced.

"I brought you acetaminophen too. Take some and lay down. No one will bother you in here. When you're ready I'll drive you home."

"Thank you."

She nodded. "Just text me whenever you're ready." She rose and walked from the room, leaving me with a plate of food, a major headache and hangover, and feelings of guilt mixed with shame.

~

I had managed to pull myself together enough in another hour for Shelby to drive me home. I didn't know if I truly felt better or I just didn't want to impose on her anymore. She had given me time to recuperate, but I could feel the energy was still focused on what I had done.

She pulled in the driveway and parked.

"Thank you again," I said.

She nodded. "Please rest up and take it easy. I'll text you later. Maybe we can do something later in break."

I stopped at the door and waited until she pulled from the driveway. I opened the door and peered inside. "Hello?" I called out. I listened for anyone to respond, but I heard nothing but the general noise of our HVAC unit. I peeked into the kitchen, but it was vacant. A note was secured to the refrigerator.

Soph-

Caleb and I went to the store, then out to the park at the center of town. Be back later. Call if you need anything.

Well, at least that was lucky. I wouldn't have to pretend I wasn't hungover to Mama's face. I could wallow in my pity, but first, I wanted to swing. I grabbed my key off the top of my bag, pulled the door shut and relocked it.

The day was chillier than it had been lately, but according to my phone, it was still in the fifties. I supposed after a string of unseasonably warm afternoons, fifty degrees could feel chilly.

I walked slowly, not wanting to aggravate my body. The breeze helped to wake me up from the hangover daze. I should have brought a sports drink with me to continue to rehydrate and replenish the nutrients my body had leeched out from the beer.

The small neighborhood playground loomed in the

distance, and I was thankful no families were taking advantage of it during spring break on a Saturday. I made a beeline for the swings and slowly sat. My head was less woozy than when I had woken up, but I didn't want to risk it.

I used my feet to push off the ground and make the swing barely move. I didn't want to tempt too much momentum, at least not at first.

Footsteps crunched the twigs as they approached.

I turned to check who it could be. No one had been around as I had walked to the park.

The familiar blond hair and black-framed glasses looked toward me. "Hey, Sophie."

I smiled. "Hey, Drew."

"Can I sit?"

"Sure. It's not my park."

Drew chuckled. "I know, but I was just checking that you were okay with some company."

"I don't mind, although I don't know how great of company I'll be for you."

"I don't care. I just wanted to make sure you were okay."

"Why … Oh, right. I forgot. I suppose I owe you a debt of gratitude."

Drew's eyebrows crinkled. "Shelby told you, I suppose."

I nodded and reached to touch his hand as he grasped the chain on the swing. "Thank you, Drew. I'm truly lucky you found me and told Shelby. It could have gone a lot worse."

"I'm glad I could help. But, honestly, Sophie, I'm worried about you."

I groaned.

"What? Are you okay? Are you in pain?"

"No, it's not that. I groaned because you're worried about me too?"

"You were really out of it last night. I had been surprised to see you drinking in the first place, but to see you passed out." He ran his fingers through his hair then adjusted his glasses. "Let's just say I don't ever want to see that again. I doubt I'll forget what it looked like as it is."

"I'm sorry. God, I've really screwed up everything."

Drew stopped moving and hovered his hand over mine before he rested it on top. The warmth from his fingers soothed me. "What's going on? I've seen it in glimpses the last few weeks. You failed a test at school, and now this? At the risk of sounding repetitive, this doesn't seem like you."

I stared blankly in front of me. He was right—they were all right—but the spinning didn't stop, and I didn't just mean from my hangover. Tears spilled over and down my cheek. I didn't even notice until Drew handed me a small piece of fabric.

I wiped my cheek and handed it back to him.

He shook his head. "You keep it, but more importantly, what's going on? I saw you last night. You were on that couch and seemed fine, and then suddenly, everything shifted, and you practically bolted from the room."

I sniffed. "It's such a long story."

He took my hand and held it between both of his. "You can tell me. I'm here."

Should I tell him what was going on? Despite our initial divide, he had truly become a person I could say I trusted. He seemed to be there—and not just in an employee and boss kind of way. "It all started with Mama announcing Rowan as her boyfriend. I was totally blindsided. She had him at breakfast, sitting at the table like he belonged there. It wasn't right. As if that wasn't bad, she replaced his picture."

Drew's brows knitted. "Your dad?"

I nodded and sniffled as a shockwave rocked through my body. "She had gotten portraits done with Rowan at the festival. Then she replaced the photo of my parents dancing when they were dating with the new portrait. She's just replacing him everywhere I turn."

"And what about last night? What happened?"

"I didn't plan on getting drunk. I planned on taking the edge off, suppressing the anger from that night. I couldn't even mention it to Caleb, because he was completely fine with it. He thought the picture was cool, and I just couldn't bare it. I decided to party, and Shelby agreed to go. I just wanted to feel buzzed—not hungover, just buzzed enough to relax and feel happy."

"And then?"

"And then that stupid song came on."

"Which song?"

"'Simple Man.'"

Drew's eyes widened, and he nodded. "Your dad's favorite song."

"Exactly. It was, like, at that moment, it was more than I could handle. I haven't heard that song in years. No one plays it; it's old. Yanno? Yet, at the party, while I tried to forget the pain, it came on over the speakers. It was like he was speaking to me, but I couldn't reply. How cruel is that, to be reminded of his absence? So, I lost it. I grabbed the beer and bolted. I certainly didn't expect to pass out, but I couldn't sit there and pretend everything was okay." My voice broke, and more tears streaked my face. I covered my face to hide the tears.

Drew's arms suddenly embraced me and held on as I sobbed into his shirt. He didn't say anything; he just slowly rubbed my back up and down as I soaked the front of his shirt.

When I finally pulled away, my hair was stuck to my face from the tears, and I could already feel the puffiness spreading to the area under my eyes. *Great, puffy and hungover, what a combination.* I patted my eyes with the fabric and raised my chin to stare into Drew's gaze.

His brown eyes were warm and full of empathy. I could see the worry in the corners and feel the concern. "I don't know how to make it better that you lost him, but this way isn't working."

"I know it isn't, but I don't know what else to do. I can't forget him, but everyone else can so easily. I just don't understand how it's so different for them than it is for me."

"Maybe it's not, but you'll never know." He looked around then back at me. "Wanna walk home? I'll go all the way to your house before I head to mine."

I sniffled again. "Okay. I should probably shower and clean up before Mama gets home anyway. I don't need her to find out about last night. She would go berserk."

Drew stood in front, as if prepared to catch me if I stumbled.

Luckily, my legs decided to cooperate. We walked a ways in silence. "Yanno, I don't know how you're so patient and kind to me. I really don't deserve it."

He stared at my purple-corded bracelet and held it in his hands. "I told you when I got you this that you deserved it. That's behind us, okay? You don't have to keep apologizing."

I stopped walking. "I know, but, Drew, I'm a mess. I have no idea what I'm doing anymore. This isn't how I want to be, but I don't know what else to do. And it's not just the past screwups. Lately, all I've been doing is hurting people I care about."

"Just take it one step at a time. Things will get better."

I snorted. "People always say time heals all, but this pain threatens to rip me apart every day. I still want him to walk through the door and pick me up, spin me around in his arms and laugh together until my stomach hurt. I still expect him to tell me a bedtime story and to hear his laugh bellow down the hallway. It's been almost six years, and I trick myself into believing it doesn't hurt quite as bad, but inside, I'm raging that he was taken from us, that he left for his job and never came home. How can time help that?"

"It may not. At some point, you'll simply learn to live with the loss. It may still spike, but we're all here for you when it does." He nudged my arm, and I continued walking.

"You should run away and never look back."

Drew chuckled but stared when I didn't laugh. "Are you serious?"

"Yes. I'm such a hot mess. I don't know how I can even be a good friend or company to anyone. You don't need this."

"You're grieving, Sophie. I won't run away just because you're going through something."

"Well, I warned you."

He shook his head. "Let's get you home so you can rest. Then you can argue your point later."

I nodded and kept walking.

Drew stayed true to his word. He walked me to my door and waited for me to enter before he left.

I locked the door and trudged to my bed. I needed to seriously figure out what I was doing with my life.

CHAPTER 20

I couldn't believe it was already Monday, with Easter break behind me. I had spent break alone, minus the few shifts at the theater, which I had managed to get Mama to drop me off and pick me up so I could avoid Riley.

I knew it would be bad when they all saw me today. I had ignored messages and calls. I had spent most of break studying or crawling into a hole in my bed. Either way, lunch would be rough.

I hurried while at my locker to prevent anyone from catching me there and sprinted to my first class—Math with Mr. Warner. The classroom was only a few hallways down, and I knew it was nowhere near Riley's or Shelby's classes.

I exhaled deeply when I sat in my seat. I piled my books on my desk and prepared my notebook with the heading on the board until someone made an announcement over the room's speaker. *"Mr. Warner, can you please send Sophie Graham to the guidance counselor's office?"*

He raised his gaze to the speaker. "Sure thing." He tilted his head toward the hallway as he stared at me.

I crammed my books into my bag and sprinted down the hallway. I had no idea why I had to go to the counselor's office, but I certainly didn't want to be late for it. The counselor's office was in the back of the building by the administration offices for the department heads. I had only visited once or twice in my entire three years at Honey Cove High. I approached the front counter.

Mrs. Young was the receptionist for all the offices in the back. She peered over her red-framed glasses as the auburn hair on the top of her head bounced in her bun. "Can I help you?"

"I was told to come see Ms. Nolan."

She typed something on her computer and nodded. "You can go back to her room. Third door on the right."

"Thank you."

She stared into the computer as if it contained a magical code to the universe.

The hallway was narrow and cluttered with boxes outside the front offices. As I approached Ms. Nolan's room, the scent of a cinnamon candle infiltrated my senses. I knocked on the half-opened door.

Ms. Nolan stood and waved me in. "Come in. Go ahead and have a seat."

I sat as she stood and closed the door—an act that set me on edge. Conversations behind closed doors were always bad.

Once she took a seat, she met my gaze. "Welcome back from spring break. I hope you had a good one?"

I nodded even though I certainly wouldn't categorize my break as a good one.

"Do you know why I've called you to my office today?"

I shook my head.

"A few of your teachers have mentioned that you've been

tardy to their classes lately, and in Physics, your last test grade is extremely out of the ordinary for you."

My stomach dropped into my feet. Of all the places I had expected to have this conversation today, it wasn't in this room—that felt more like a closet than an actual office.

She peered over the screen of her computer. "Is everything going okay with you?"

"Yeah."

She eyed me warily. "Sophie, I have your record with us up, and you've barely sneezed the wrong way since you've been here. It's obvious that your pattern is different lately, and I just want to ensure everything is okay with you."

"I guess it's just college stress."

Ms. Nolan grabbed a pen from her cup and scribbled something on a Post-it Note. "This feels a little different than college stress." She tapped the pen as I stayed silent. "You know, if you can't be honest with me, I'll have no choice but to call your mother to find out."

My jaw slackened. "Is that really necessary? It was just one test."

"It's less about the test and more about your overall demeanor. Many of the teachers have shown concern that you aren't your normal self. In your age, we just want to ensure nothing is happening to you that would cause you to do anything drastic."

I raised an eyebrow in response. "Drastic? Like what?"

She fidgeted with the pen. "We don't want you to end up harming yourself."

My eyes widened. "I'm not suicidal."

"Well, that's good to hear, but these are classic signs of something going on. If it's not that, then what?"

I sighed. I certainly didn't expect to tell my guidance counselor everything, but I also didn't want them to call Mama and get me in trouble. Without another idea, I decided the truth was the best option. "My mama is dating again. It's been almost six years since my dad died, and I'm struggling with the change."

Ms. Nolan tapped the pen to her lip. "I see. Have you discussed this with her?"

I shook my head. "She seems happy, but I feel worse the further it gets."

"Does he hurt you?"

"What? No."

"Okay, sorry. I had to ask. So, is he a decent man?"

I nodded. "It appears so. She's happy, and my brother likes him, but he doesn't remember my dad as much as I do. She even replaced a photo of them dancing with her new boyfriend."

"Sophie, are you worried she's forgetting about your dad and then will forget about you?"

"I think so."

"Or are you more worried about what it means if you end up liking this guy, what happens to the memories of your dad?"

I nodded as tears welled.

"I can't possibly imagine the pain you feel, but I do know that when we lose someone, like our father, we aren't tainting their memory if we move on. It's okay to miss him every day and still like being around her boyfriend. It doesn't have to be one or the other."

"It just feels like a betrayal to my dad's memory. It's doesn't feel right that he died doing his job and we just keep going on. It should have just been the three of us forever once he died."

Ms. Nolan tilted her head. "You would want your mom to be alone for the rest of her life? Decades?"

"Well, no. Not if you put it like that. But someone else to love doesn't feel right."

She drummed her fingers on the table. "I'm not saying you must do this, because no one can make you, but I think you need to have an open and honest conversation with her. Whether you believe it or not, she probably still deals with her own grief and is a good person to lean on as you continue to navigate your own."

"She just seems fine. I don't know that I want to bring her down if she's okay."

"She's your mom, Sophie. Moms are there to help their children. She won't be upset with you if you admit you're struggling with your dad being gone. She can only help what she knows about."

I sighed. "That makes sense, but I don't know if I even know how to fully explain it to her. I barely have my own head wrapped around it."

"Even just sharing what you shared with me will help. I can understand your behavior more clearly now. I still must urge you to pay more attention to your time management, because you don't want to ruin your record, but I think its leaching into school, because you can't deal with it at home. Try it out and see how it goes. If it helps, that's wonderful. If not, we can discuss more strategies. How does that sound?"

"I think that works."

Ms. Nolan smiled. "Getting older is never easy, but I think you'll be surprised to see who you have in your corner if you just let them. I'll call you back in a week or so and see how you're doing. If you need more before then, just let Mrs. Young know, and we can schedule it sooner, okay?"

I nodded. "Thank you, Ms. Nolan."

"It's my job. I hope things get sorted out for you, Sophie."

I grabbed my bag from the floor and stood. "Me too."

I checked the time on the wall and noticed I still had ten more minutes in Math. I sprinted back to class to hopefully catch him before he left. I would have to find out what I had missed and get caught up, but, for the first time in many days, the weight on my shoulders felt a little lighter.

~

I stared at the double doors leading to the cafeteria. I dreaded going to lunch, only because I didn't want a lecture from everyone. Riley hadn't had a chance to yell at me in person, and, after ghosting her and Shelby over Easter break, I knew I would hear it.

I inhaled deeply and opened the door to see Shelby, Riley, and Randy sitting at the table. I gulped loudly and strolled toward them.

They all faced me as I approached.

Riley's expression changed to a scowl.

Yep, definitely was going to hear it.

Shelby crossed her arms and watched as I sat next to her.

"Hey, guys."

Riley huffed. "Hey, guys? Are you serious? I'm so mad at you, I could throw something at your head."

My eyes widened. "Okay. Well, I'm here, so let me have it."

Randy shook his head as if to say that was a poor choice of words.

"You completely lied to us when you said you wouldn't drink. You scared Shelby and I half to death when you had to be carried from another party. Then you completely ignored our texts. What's with that? Are you trying to isolate yourself?"

"I'm sorry. I didn't know how to deal with what I was feeling. It wasn't the smartest way to handle it, and I owe you both. Can you forgive me?"

Riley folded her arms and blew air out her nose in puffs. "I'm too mad at you. I can't forgive you at this second."

Randy eyed all three of us. "Are you okay, Sophie? Like,

really okay? It's a dangerous spiral to go down. Trust me, I know."

I gasped. "Oh my god, Randy. I'm so sorry. I didn't even think about how much it would impact you too. I promise I never meant to stick vinegar in a wound."

Randy smiled weakly. "I know you didn't, Sophie. I just don't want to see you end up the way my dad has. It's not a pleasant journey if you keep down that road."

"I swear I won't drink again."

Shelby's eyebrows knitted. "How do we even trust you? You told us that after last time. This could be another trick to set us up later."

I shook my head. "No. I understand a little better what is happening with me. I won't go in that direction." I fiddled with my brown bag. "Ms. Nolan called me to her office."

"Ms. Nolan? Why would she want to see you?" Riley asked.

"My teachers have apparently noticed a change in me and told her. She asked what the deal was, and when I said it was college stress, she flat out didn't believe me."

Riley uncrossed her arms. "Sophie, what *is* happening with you?"

Shelby reached for my hand. "We're here. You can tell us anything you know."

I nodded. "It's hard for me to share that kind of pain. I'm used to dealing with it on my own. I don't know how to talk to people about it, and I guess that's what has been overflowing. I drank to avoid the feelings. But Ms. Nolan helped me figure out a plan. I'm going to try that."

"Well, plan or no plan, we're here for you, Sophie. We're mad because we care. I don't want something to happen to you like that. No matter what your pain is, you can set some of it on us," Riley said.

I looked to each of them as they nodded. "That means a

lot, you guys. I can't promise I'll be good at sharing everything all the time, but it means a lot for you all to be here for me if I need it."

Now all I had to do was tell Mama, and that was scarier than this conversation times one hundred.

CHAPTER 21

I twisted the fabric of my lanyard around my finger. I was beyond nervous to have this conversation with Mama. I had no idea how it would go, but, at this point, I knew it needed to happen.

Mama stood at the sink washing dishes.

I inched closed, carefully, deciding how to even start.

"Do you need something, Sophie?" she asked without turning around.

"How'd you know it was me?"

Mama chuckled. "I'm your mama. I know both of you, and I could feel you staring at me for the past three minutes, so there must be something you want to discuss." She peered over her shoulder and stared at my face. "Yep. Definitely need to talk." She dried her hands on the dishtowel and gestured to the kitchen table.

I nodded and sat.

"Is everything okay? You look so serious."

I shook my head.

Mama scooted her chair closer. "What is it?"

"I-I need to talk to you about Rowan ... and Dad."

Mama's eyes widened, but she stayed silent.

"I haven't been honest about everything. I'm still not over Dad dying. I still have dreams about him being in the kitchen and laughing with us. I still picture him walking through the door." My voice hitched. "I still talk to him and wish he was here. And I don't know how to feel that and make room for someone else. It feels like you're replacing him with Rowan. You took down his picture."

Mama grabbed my hand and squeezed. "Sophie, I don't ever expect you to *get over* your father. I still have those moments too."

My eyes widened as I stared into her gaze. "You do?"

"Of course, Sophie. He was my husband, my love." Mama sighed. "I guess I haven't done a good job of showing you my own grief." Mama wrapped me in a tight squeeze and rubbed my arm. "No one, not even Rowan, could ever replace your dad. He gave me you and Caleb, and that bond will never diminish. I loved him so fiercely, but I also know he would never want me to stay a widow. He would want someone around for Caleb, to show him the ropes, and for you, to show you love as you get older." Mama handed me a tissue. "We had talked about it. When he enlisted, we knew what could happen. We knew the risk. He would laugh and tell me that if something happened to him, I should move on. I thought he was crazy, and I told him I would never do that. I would never forget him or love someone else like I loved him." She shook her head. "He would nod but with that smirk, like he knew better."

"I think I remember what you mean."

"It isn't fair you two lost your dad so young. I was so angry at first; it consumed me. I hated that he left us."

I gasped from the wave of emotion that hit me. "Me too. I still do get mad. He should still be here. He should be showing Caleb how to throw a baseball and what to do on sports teams. He should explain how to treat women."

Mama brushed her finger over my cheek. "He should be here for you as you navigate boys."

The tears slid down out of my control. "Mama, I just don't know what to do with this feeling anymore. I suppressed it, and it resurfaced so much stronger. I resent Rowan for who he replaces. I know he makes you happy, and I know he's a good guy." I lowered my head into my hands. "But he isn't Dad."

Mama rubbed my back and sighed. "I wish you would have told me this sooner, Sophie. I could have helped you. Honestly, I should have expected it based on your reactions."

I shrugged. "It's hard to know if I don't tell you."

"True, but I also should have remembered that losing your dad wasn't an easy thing and that it could come back and rear its head at any time in your life. I suspect this won't be the only time you struggle with that fact. It will reoccur as you grow older and experience life without him. But more importantly, I forgot to remind you that we can always have more love for others. You don't have a finite amount that is only allotted to a few. It's okay to love others and still love your dad. I mean, you've opened yourself up to not one but *two* new friends this year. I'm so proud of you for that."

"What, Riley and Shelby? That's not the same."

"No, it isn't, but it's a start."

I swiped the back of my hand over my eyes. "Ugh, I'm tired of crying. I'm tired of screwing up."

Mama's eyebrows rose. "Screwing up?"

"I got called to the guidance counselor's office today. Ms. Nolan warned me about my record at school. With being tardy and a poor test grade, they're concerned. And I know what you're going to say; I will fix it. I know I will, but I don't know how to control the spillage from Dad to everything else. I feel like I'm unwinding, and I don't know how to stop."

"Oh, sweetie. I know you'll fix it. That's how you are, but I wish I had known it was impacting you so much. I guess I've been so preoccupied with everything else that I didn't take the time to notice. You sent all the signs, especially when you got drunk, that I should have pushed harder. You've always kept your head on your shoulders, so I figured it must have been you acting out because of Rowan, which probably was true, but so much deeper than that."

I nodded. "I just liked not feeling the pain of losing Dad. But it happened the second time, the Friday I stayed at Shelby's. I might have gotten drunk again. I heard 'Simple Man' on the speakers, and I lost control. I didn't plan to get drunk again, but it just happened." I stared into Mama's gaze. "It was his song. It's like, I can't handle his memories, and I can't handle not having them at the same time."

She nodded. "I know what you mean. It's a bittersweet thing, but you must remember he loved you so much, Sophie. When I'm really down, I think what would he want me to do? How would he want me to live? And I don't think he would want you or us to go through this half-life because he died."

"I'm sure you're right, but it's so hard. Every time I move past and I feel fine, something pops up and makes me start all over. How can I miss him so desperately and still be happy and move on?"

"It takes time and understanding that being happy wouldn't upset him. Your dad never liked seeing you two hurt, and for you to hurt because of him would crush him. You have to live, truly live, to honor his memory."

"I like to think I usually do, maybe not lately, but I do."

Mama eyed me warily.

"What?"

"You've closed yourself off so completely to outside love that I worry about you."

I sniffled. "What do you mean?"

"Drew likes you—or, at least, could like you."

My eyes widened. "What? Why would you say that?"

"And I think you like him too. But I'd imagine you have such a wall up around your heart you haven't even realized it yet."

Did I like Drew? "I think I would know if I cared about someone."

Mama shook her head. "That's where I disagree. You're so focused on the losses you've already had you can't see where you could be happy with a boy who wears glasses."

"What makes you think he likes me?"

"Mama's intuition. The day he spent with us at lunch, you softened up. You relaxed and even let your guard down around us. I haven't seen you that carefree since Rowan came into the picture."

"I-I don't know, Mama. I doubt he could like me after what happened when we were younger. He had a crush then, and I didn't respond well."

"You mean the summer after your dad died? Sophie, of course you didn't. You had just lost someone you cared deeply for. What if you had let your heart open up and it got crushed? That's normal, but it doesn't mean it'll happen. I would worry less about how he feels and decide how you do. If you can't be honest with yourself, you can't be honest with anyone else."

I nodded and inhaled deeply. "What do I do next?"

"I'm not sure, that depends on you, but I do think, for us, we need to do something else. I don't want you to feel like you can't talk to me about your dad. I'm always here for you, no matter who I'm with. I'll ease up with Rowan until we figure out what feels okay for you."

"I don't want you to break up with him. You deserve to be happy too."

Mama smiled weakly. "I won't break up with him, but I won't force interactions as much. I'll wait until you feel like you're ready. I should have done that to begin with. I was selfish, because I wanted you two to meet him and love him like I do. I just wanted your lives to be brighter too."

I squeezed Mama's hand. "Well, thank you for listening."

"Always. Oh, and you are absolutely grounded for the time being until we get your grades up and I can trust where you're going."

I nodded. "That's fair." I smiled, stood then meandered down the hallway as I stared at our family photos. The people in them felt like a completely different family even though I could remember most of those times.

I closed the door to my room and sat on the bed. There was so much to process from our conversation that I had no idea where to begin.

I pulled up the group text on my phone and sent a message. *I talked to Mama about it all. I'm grounded, which I figured, but it was nice to tell her and not keep it bottled up.*

Riley: *That's great, Sophie. I'm glad you did it.*

Shelby: *How do you feel?*

I'm not sure, to be honest. Mama and the counselor today made some good points. They said I wall myself off to protect my heart from future hurt. Also that I can make room for others and still have a special place for my dad.

Riley: *That makes sense. We can always add to our village.*

Shelby: *Do you agree with what they said though? Or does it feel like it doesn't fit?*

I can certainly be prickly and walled off, so it isn't that farfetched.

Shelby: *What will you do next?*

I have no idea. I need to figure out my school stuff first, then I guess see how it goes? I might journal when I feel things about Dad to see if it helps. I really don't know. I never expected to feel like this after so much time had passed.

Riley: *I'm so proud of you, Sophie. We're here for you if you need anything. You can always talk to us about it.*

I know I can, after today at lunch.

Shelby: *Do you need anything right now?*

I don't think so. I do need your opinions on something.

Riley: *Anything.*

Shelby: *Go ahead.*

Mama brought up Drew. She said she thinks he likes me ... and that I like him back.

Riley: *Well, what do you think about that?*

He can't like me. We've just started talking again and being normal.

Shelby: *Yes, but does it feel like friends when you're around him, or does it feel like it's so much more important than that?*

I have no idea. We haven't spent that much time together other than at work.

Shelby: *Didn't you spend like the whole festival with him after your shift?*

Well, yeah, and my family.

Riley: *So, how did it feel?*

I have no idea! That's why I'm asking you two.

Riley: *We can't answer that for you. You must decide how you feel.*

Ugh! Y'all sound like fortune cookies. Can't you just tell me what you see?

Shelby: *Is your question if he could care about you or if you could care about him as more than friends?*

I guess both.

Riley: *He likes you.*

Shelby: *He likes you.*

Riley: *Ha! Jinx.*

Shelby: *But, Sophie, we can't tell* you *how to feel. You must figure that out, and if you're honestly wondering about how he feels, why don't you have that conversation with him too?*

My eyes widened. Talk to him about it? Definitely not, that sounded like a horrible idea. I had enough instability without trying to figure out a completely different relationship.

Maybe.

CHAPTER 22

$\mathcal{I}$ stared at the popcorn popping and wished it was more exciting, like a mad rush of people or magic animals.

Magic animals? I was really bored.

"Still no one?" Drew asked.

I shook my head. "I've never been so bored in my entire life. I've stared at the popcorn for what feels like forever. Everything is restocked, nothing else to make. I can't deal."

Drew chuckled. "You'll survive. I'll be back."

I nodded and watched as he walked away from the snack counter. I might as well get out my physics book if it was going to be this slow. I promised Mama my grades would improve, and Physics was the worst one.

I flipped the pages until I found the right chapter on energy. I sighed and stared at the words. Things like kinetic, potential, and mechanical flung out to my face, and I exhaled deeply. This chapter was full of vocabulary, and thanks to my inattentiveness, I not only didn't remember the lectures in class, but I also hadn't done any of the reading.

I straightened and cracked my fingers. I could do this. I

just needed to focus and pay attention to the words on the page. I surveyed the lobby one more time before I hung my head and read as much as I could manage.

"Whatcha doing?" Drew asked.

I startled. "You can't do that to someone!"

Drew chuckled. "I figured you would have heard me. I lugged, like, four boxes behind the counter."

I looked up and realized Drew was right. Four boxes surrounded the area by my ankles. "Oh. I didn't even hear you."

"Apparently." Drew leaned closer and peeked over my shoulder. "Physics? Oh, you're trying to get your grade up."

I nodded. "And I think I'm going cross-eyed. There are so many types of energy; how am I possibly supposed to remember them all?"

"That's easy. Look at the prefixes, suffixes, and roots of the words. Most, if not all, give it away."

I set my right hand on my hip and stared. "Right. If I could figure that out, I wouldn't need to stare at the page like it was translated from Greek to Russian and then to English."

Drew shook his head. "You're being dramatic." Drew waved his arms around his head as fast as he could.

"What are you doing?"

"What are my arms doing?"

"Moving, obviously. Are you okay? Did you have a stroke?"

"No. What type of energy deals with motion?"

I sighed. "I have no idea."

"It's kinetic. Kinetic comes from the Greek word kinētikos, which means *of motion*."

I rolled my eyes. "How the heck do you remember that?"

He shrugged. "I just do." He leaned over the book once more. "What does potential mean?"

I stared. "I don't know."

"Sophie, think about it. If someone has potential. What does it mean?"

"They have the chance to do something?"

Drew grinned. "Exactly! And potential energy has the chance or the *potential* to do work."

I raised an eyebrow. "Okay, well that one makes sense, but there are several others."

"Take it one at a time, and you'll get there."

"I hope so. If I don't fix my grade, I'll be grounded until I graduate, maybe longer."

Drew took a boxcutter from the counter and sliced open the box closest to me. "She found out about the test?"

"I told her. After everything that had happened, Ms. Nolan called me to her office."

Drew's eyebrows knitted. "Wow. I've never been to her office."

"Neither had I, but I guess things change." I bent to help him stack the candy boxes next to us. "Anyway, the talk was good, actually helpful. I went home and told my mama everything—how I had gotten drunk again, my grades, my dad, and Rowan. I laid it all out on the table."

"Impressive. How'd she take it?"

"Not too bad. She grounded me, obviously, but that's to be expected. She agreed to go a little slower with Rowan and wait until I expressed my comfort with certain steps. She also told me she still misses my dad. I guess I just never picked up on her own grief through mine."

"I'm glad it went well, Sophie. That's great news."

I nodded. "Me too. But it's so much harder picking up the pieces than it was stomping all over the place and creating them."

Drew chuckled. "That may be true, but studying is definitely a good start. You can only take baby steps. It wasn't one instant that caused the crumble, so it won't be one instant that fixes it all."

I looked up and smiled.

His eyes were warm and comforting brown. His hair fell just over the frame of his glasses.

Little tingles erupted in my stomach, and goosebumps dispersed across my arm.

"I can help you study if you help me stack these boxes."

I stuck out my hand. "Deal."

He shook it, and the heat from his hand made my belly do a shimmy.

What the heck was happening? Was this a sign I liked him? No. That couldn't be; something must have bothered my stomach from lunch. That's all it was. Right?

"Okay. So, we left off with potential. Do you remember the two types?"

I shook my head as I moved a stack of gummy bears from the floor to the counter.

"Think about how something could gain energy, to wind up for it."

I stared into the distance, hoping something would click.

Drew stared at me as he stretched a rubber band over and over again.

"What's with the rubber band?"

"It's to help. As I stretch back the rubber band, I'm putting in energy for it to use later. This is called elastic potential energy."

"Oh. So, if something is stretched or compressed it will store energy?"

Drew clapped. "Yes! So, springs work in a similar way. When you compress them closed, it causes the energy to be stored until you release it."

"Okay, well that is easy then."

"And what about the other type?"

"No idea."

Drew took the candy boxes and stacked them above our heads on a shelf.

I cocked my head to the side. "So, I get you're trying to clue me in, but I can't think. How does the height matter in potential energy?"

"If the shelf disappeared magically, what happens?"

"The candy falls."

"Why?"

I looked at him as if he was five and asking stupid questions. "Because of gravity, obviously. It pulls everything down." I gasped. "Oh! Does gravity have to do with the second type?"

He nodded. "Gravitational potential energy. When I move something to the shelf, I'm raising it from the ground up higher and, therefore, transferring the energy it takes to move it into the object. As it goes higher, the more energy it has, because gravity will pull it back when the object that is holding it releases it."

"Hmm. That's practical."

"Yep. That's why I like it. It all makes sense. It has reasons for why the world works the way it does."

I eyed him warily. "Don't tell me physics is your favorite?"

Drew smirked. "Maybe. Or maybe it's one of them."

I shook my head. "I should have known."

"It's just nice to have the predictability of it. Energy is all around us. You have energy in appliances from electrical energy. Have you heard of thermal shirts before?"

I nodded. "They keep you warm."

"Exactly! Thermal energy is about heat, how fast the particles are moving. The faster they move, the hotter it is, the more thermal energy. When you bake a cake, the ingredients change through chemical energy. Nuclear energy with the *nucleus* of a cell. It all comes together."

I giggled. "Okay, okay. I see your point. I'll need you to say those again, but slower this time. And also maybe not so much geeking out?"

He rolled his eyes. "I wasn't being a geek."

I laughed. "Oh, yes you were, but it was sweet."

"Mm-hmm, sure. Because any guy wants to hear a pretty girl call them a geek?"

My eyes widened, and heat crawled up my cheeks. "A pretty girl?"

Drew waved me off. "You know you're pretty. Anyway, we have two more boxes to unpack, then I'll help you study more."

I nodded, but my brain could only focus on the fact he had called me pretty. Was everyone right about the situation and I was completely oblivious? Was that possible?

CHAPTER 23

*R*iley set the cake pan into the oven and fixed the timer for thirty minutes. "I hope this chocolate cake turns out okay."

"You and me both. I can't afford to have my grade in foods class fall apart."

Riley wiped her hand on her apron and sat on the stool. "Well, the good thing is we have time to catch up while the cake bakes."

I pulled over a stool. "Very true. How was your date over break? With everything going on, I never got a chance to ask."

Riley beamed. "It was nice. We drove around and talked. Then we went to Over Easy's. It wasn't anything crazy, but it was absolutely perfect for me."

I smiled. "I'm glad it went well. Are things all good now between the two of you?"

She nodded. "I was brave, and I told him how I had felt. He said that with the festival being over, he would have more time. Not too much, because since the festival was a hit, they'll have to have another one. But in the meantime, it isn't quite so crazy."

"That's good. You can relax a little more now."

"Yes. I felt so silly asking him those things, but he was a gentleman, like always. He caressed my cheek and told me that he only had eyes for me." She sighed in that lovesick kind of way. "It was so sweet."

I gagged. "How splendid."

Riley punched my arm. "Whatever. When you admit feelings for Drew, you'll be just as bad. Then Shelby and I'll make fun of you."

"Hey, first of all, it's playful banter. I don't actually mean it. Secondly, who says I'll be like you two?"

Riley's eyebrow rose. "Wait, you didn't deny feelings for Drew." She gasped and covered her mouth with her hand. "So, you like him? You're admitting it?"

I crossed my arms. "I don't know what I'm admitting. My stomach gets all weird around him, and my hands get clammy. It could just be a weird allergy to the theater."

Riley dramatically rolled her eyes. "You did *not* just say that. An allergy? Sophie, those are signs of a crush on someone. You don't have an allergy; you like him!"

"Keep your voice down, would you? I don't need the whole class spreading gossip they know nothing about."

Riley lowered her voice. "Fine, but it's not an allergy. You like him; he likes you. When ya gonna do something about it?"

"You are so pushy, yanno?"

Riley giggled. "It's fun. I think I like this side of it more than I like my normal side. You get to have so much fun teasing me. I see why you do it. But seriously, if he likes you and you like him, why not see where things go? You aren't in middle school anymore."

"My life is a hot mess, Riley. How can I possibly jump into a relationship right now?"

"No one is saying to marry the kid. I'm saying to see what you guys have in common. Go on a date and see where you end up. Dates feel different when feelings are all out there. It's more special and monumental if it gets messed up."

I gulped. "Yeah, sounds like no pressure at all."

"It's only pressure if you make it pressurized. You both have a lot to relearn about each other. Why can't you do that and still admit there is a spark between you two? That's all I'm saying."

Riley made it sound so easy, as if telling him how I felt wouldn't change everything. The expectations alone would ruin everything. No, he didn't need to be dragged into my drama any more than he already had been. Sure, I liked him, I guessed, but I didn't have to admit to it—at least not to him anyway. I liked the ease between us now. The twinge of guilt every time I was near him had disappeared, and I could finally remember what it had been like to have him as a friend. I didn't want that screwed up, because I *could* like him.

Our oven dinged, and Riley checked it with her toothpick. "Looks done." She pulled it from the oven and let it cool. "Once it's cool enough, we can add the frosting."

I licked my lips. "Are you sure I can't just eat the frosting by itself?"

"No, and just for that, I'm moving it over here. I don't need our cake to have no frosting and we lose points."

I held up my hands in defense. "I won't take the frosting, but it's certainly tempting."

Riley stuck out her tongue, and we focused on the remaining steps of our recipe. Class would be over soon, and it had to be finished today.

I carried my half of the cake and wandered to Ms. Nolan's office. I had an opening period after Food's, and I wanted to check in with her.

Mrs. Young sat glued to her computer screen as I approached the desk.

"Can I see Ms. Nolan?"

Mrs. Young looked up, clicked a few things on her keyboard then met my gaze again. "Go on back. She should be available."

"Thank you."

The hallway was still overcrowded with stuff, but it didn't seem quite so stifling as last time. I knocked once I reached her door.

"Come in!" she shouted.

I carefully eased open the door.

"Ah, Sophie. How are you?" She gestured to the chair. "Come sit." She sniffed the air. "Oh, is that the chocolate cake from foods class? I have to always avoid that hallway during this lesson. It just smells positively amazing."

"Would you like some? There's no way I'll eat it all."

She hesitated, as if debating whether to agree or not. "No, that's okay. I really shouldn't." She straightened her posture and looked directly into my eyes. "How can I help you?"

"I wanted to come back and thank you. I didn't know how much I needed that push to talk to my mama. I went home that day, and we sat and talked about it all."

"That's wonderful news, Sophie. How did it feel to do that?"

"It felt like I lifted a rather large weight off my shoulders. I know it doesn't cure everything, and I certainly will need more time to figure things out, but it felt like a good start."

"I'm so glad to hear that. How have your classes been going?"

I tilted my head back and forth. "Okay. It won't be a quick fix, especially for Physics, but I take as much time as I can to study for that class. I'm hoping I do well on the next quiz. You were right; it'll take me the rest of the semester to fix the grade, but at least it's a start in the right direction."

Ms. Nolan smiled. "You certainly seem to be better. A little more balanced today, would you agree?"

I nodded. "I think the weight of holding it all in made it hard to react to anything else that happened. It all snowballed, and I didn't know how to stop the momentum."

Ms. Nolan leaned back in her chair. "I think you have a great future as long as you continue this new path. I'm here anytime, okay, Sophie? If you ever need to talk or anything, I can certainly be here." She rummaged in her desk and retrieved a few pamphlets. "Our school doesn't have a good support team for students who have lost their parents or a loved one. However, these brochures might spark a few ideas that can help. I ultimately also recommend finding a support group that meets about grief."

"But it's been so long since it had happened."

She smiled. "That's okay, Sophie. Everyone's grief manifests itself differently and in different stages in your life. No one can tell you exactly how to deal with your dad's death, especially with your age when it happened. There is no one-size-fits-all for grief. Whatever you experience, that's what is right for you. Don't feel like you aren't grieving the correct way because it doesn't match what you see others do or heard on social media."

I nodded. "Thank you, Ms. Nolan." I slid the cake dish on the desk and opened the lid. "Are you sure you don't want any? You've helped me so much, and I appreciate that."

Ms. Nolan breathed deeply and eyed the knife inside the pan. "One little bite wouldn't hurt."

I smiled and cut her a small piece then set it on a tissue. "I'll check out these pamphlets." I stood and waved to Ms. Nolan. "I'll see you later."

"Goodbye, Sophie."

I walked to the door and started to close it as Ms. Nolan licked the frosting off the top part of the cake.

I stifled a giggle as the door shut, and I walked back past Mrs. Young.

The wall clock said today's final period would end in five minutes. I walked toward my locker. All in all, it seemed like a good start to fixing things.

CHAPTER 24

I set my half of the cake on the floor as I opened my locker. Suddenly, from the corner of my eye, the cake appeared to float next to me.

"What in the …?" I turned to see that the cake was not floating but was being held by Drew. "You freaked me out. I couldn't see you, but I could see the cake floating."

Drew smirked. "This smells so good."

I grinned. "It turned out fairly well. You want a piece?"

He eyed the cake and looked back at me. "Maybe. But that's not why I stopped."

I tilted my head to the side. "Oh?"

He shook his head. "I was hoping we could talk. Maybe we could go to Over Easy's or something?"

"Nope. I can't. I'm grounded, remember?"

"Right. Well, what if I drive you home?"

I shrugged. "Okay. I'll text Riley so she knows."

Drew smiled and nodded.

I closed the locker and rummaged in my bookbag for my phone. I typed the text and hit Send. *Drew is driving me home. I'll text you later. He wants to* talk *about something.*

"All set. Do you need to go to your locker?"

"Nope. Already went."

We strolled toward the front door.

This weird energy floated from Drew; whatever he wanted to discuss had him seeming nervous about something. My stomach dropped. Was it about the theater? Was he here to tell me Mr. Martin didn't want me working anymore?

I bit the corner of my lip. "So, what did you want to talk about?"

He shook his head. "It's so loud in the hallway; it'll be easier once we're in my car."

I scanned the nearly vacant hallway. "Ookaay."

Once outside, I slowed my pace and tilted my head to the sun.

"What are you doing?"

I gazed into his face. "This feels so amazing. The warmth from the sun, it's such a beautiful day."

Drew chuckled. "Did you hit your head? It's spring; of course, there is warmth from the sun."

I playfully glared at him. "I like to run, so warmth ignites my soul."

"Sure. Are you getting in?"

I looked down and realized we were standing right at Drew's car.

He unlocked it, and I hopped in and set my bag on the floor.

The car looked like it always did—free from any trash or leftover bottles or wrappers on the floorboards. I still didn't know if he never ate in there or if he always just kept it immaculate.

"Do you eat in your car?" I blurted.

Drew's brows knitted together. "What? Why would you ask that?"

I shrugged. "It always seems so tidy. Shouldn't a guy's car be like a bomb went off?"

"Not all guys are slobs, Sophie."

"Fair point. So … do you eat in the car?"

"Not generally. If I'm in a rush, sometimes."

So, he was just a neat person. *Hmm.*

"So, what's up?" I asked as I watched the greenery blur past the window.

Drew stayed quiet as he obsessively adjusted his glasses.

"You're freaking me out. Is something wrong?"

He faced me then re-averted his gaze to the road. "No. Sorry, I was just concentrating on driving."

"Oh. Okay."

Why was he being so weird? Whether he was admitting it yet or not, something was going on. He had asked to talk to me, and yet, he was avoiding the whole *talking* part. It made no sense.

I shifted in the seat to lean toward the window. If he wouldn't offer up what was on his mind, then I would wait. Even though the longer the silence lasted, the more my stomach did flips. I couldn't help shaking the feeling that things were about to change, and I had no idea what that meant.

Drew pulled into my driveway and took the key from the ignition.

Was he planning on coming in?

I checked the driveway, but it appeared no one else was home, except maybe Caleb. I grabbed my bag off the floorboard and got out.

Drew followed me out as well and fiddled with his car keys as he walked behind me to the front door.

I turned back. "Are you coming in?"

He shook his head. "No. But, Sophie, I need to talk to you."

I set my bookbag on the ground and focused on his face. "Okay, what's up?"

"I need to tell you something."

My eyebrows knitted together. "Okay."

"When I walked into Mr. Martin's office that first day and realized you were the one shadowing me, my stomach dropped."

My eyes widened, but I stayed silent.

"I hadn't been around you in a close environment in five years, and it terrified me. We would avoid eye contact in the hallway, and I thought you didn't want to be anywhere near me. I was surprised you were so adamant in staying to shadow me." Drew combed his fingers through his hair and pushed his glasses up his nose.

My hands became clammy. Where was he going with this?

"I'm glad you stayed. I'm glad we can discuss what had happened and move past it." He moved closer to me and grabbed my right hand. "I'm glad we've hung out again. I really missed you."

I smiled. "I missed you too."

"But there's more. When I admitted before about what happened, I left out the confirmation that I did like you. I still do, Sophie. I thought that with time, I had lost those feelings, but, when I saw you with that older couple and at the party, I realized they had never left, only been ignored. And I'm hoping that maybe this time you have feelings for me too."

"I-I ..." My throat felt as if it closed and was replaced by the Sahara Desert. He had feelings for me? Shelby and Riley were right, but what should I say? My life was a mess right now. He didn't deserve that. "Drew, things are complicated right now."

He stroked my cheek with his thumb. "Sophie, I'm not

worried about everything going on. I like you. I want to be here to help you, and if I must wait, I will. I want to know how you feel. Do you like me too?"

I tilted my head down as I looked at our feet. "I don't know what to say, Drew."

He tilted my head back up and stared into my eyes. "If you say you don't like me that way, I'll drop it. I'll just be friends with you, but if there's a chance, I just want to know."

I nibbled the inside of my lip. "I'm not good at this."

"Good at what?"

I sighed. "I don't know how to like someone, Drew. I don't let guys in, since my dad. I don't know how to manage romantic feelings for someone else."

A grin spread from the left side of his face. "Does that mean you have feelings to manage?"

I looked down and nodded.

"I can handle that." Drew bent down to meet my gaze. A broad smile spread across his face. "Sophie, I like you, and I'm okay with going on this journey with you. We can take it as slow as you want. I just want to be around you." He raised my fingers to his lips and gently kissed each one. "You're so special to me."

I exhaled a jagged breath. Each kiss sent sensations through my body I didn't recognize. "I don't understand how, after everything, you can have feelings for me."

"I thought I had moved past it, but being near you, especially at the festival, brought those feelings back ten-fold. You are such an incredible person, Sophie. I just hope you can see yourself through my eyes. You have gone through something tragic, but it doesn't make you less worthy of love. If anything, you deserve it more."

"So, what does this mean?"

Drew smiled tenderly as he stroked my cheek. "It means

I'm here for you. And when you aren't grounded anymore, it means we spend time together and see where it takes us."

I nodded. "Okay."

Drew picked me up and embraced me in a hug as he swung me around.

The action surprised me, and I burst into giggles as I let my neck relax and fall into his embrace. I hadn't realized admitting feelings for someone and having that reciprocated could feel this way.

Drew set me down and gazed into my eyes. "I should leave before I get you in trouble, but see you tomorrow?"

"I'll be the girl wearing the purple bracelet."

Drew grinned from ear to ear then leaned in and brushed his lips against my cheek. "I'll see you later, Sophie."

I nodded and watched as he got into his car and pulled from the driveway. My heart fluttered, and heat crawled up my cheeks. Shelby and Riley would freak out when I told them. But for now, I wanted to savor it all for myself.

CHAPTER 25

It took several weeks before Mama released me from my punishment. In that time, I snuck moments with Drew at the theater or in the hallways. We occasionally held hands or embraced, but we never went further. He knew I still had to adjust to everything, and I adored how much he attended to my needs.

Mama had kept to her word about going slower with Rowan. I had only seen him pick her up to go out a few times since our conversation. I still wasn't as settled with the decision of her moving on, but at least I didn't resent Rowan anymore.

I also finally finished my trial period at the theater. Mr. Martin asked me to join the staff without having to shadow anyone. I had surprised myself with how excited I was to be an actual employee, but I was also proud. I might not have started the job for all the right reasons, but I had earned that position, and now I didn't have to worry about it. The only downside was I didn't always have the same shifts as Drew.

Hands waved in front of my face. "Sophie, are you in there?"

"What? Yeah, I'm listening, Riley."

Riley put her hands on her hips, exchanged glances with Shelby and shook her head. "You were not. You were so far down the rabbit hole you totally missed what we said, and trust me, you would have reacted."

I eyed them both warily. "Well, now you have my absolute attention, because that sounds ominous."

Shelby giggled. "It isn't ominous, but you must hurry up and get finished dressing. Drew will be here soon to pick you up for your *date*."

"Why do you have to say it like that?" I asked.

"Because you, out of all of us, are going on an official date. We are proud and jealous."

Riley rolled her eyes. "I go on dates with Randy, so I don't know what you're talking about."

"Dates with feelings but as friends is not an official date. They are going out with the possibility of being boyfriend and girlfriend. Totally different."

My eyebrow rose. "You two are crazy. This is the first time we can actually spend quality time together without sneaking it or only having a car ride trip home."

"Yeah, and you two are so smitten that if he doesn't ask you out, I might injure him," Riley said.

"So much talk for someone who should be saying that to Randy," Shelby said as she wiggled her eyebrows.

"You two are too much. Why did I have you over while I got ready? You're not helping."

"Of course, we are. Who else would do your makeup if I didn't?" Shelby asked.

"I'm capable. I just choose not to. Drew knows what I look like."

"Yeah, but making yourself up can be fun," Riley said. "Where are you two going?"

"He was tightlipped about it all, but I don't care. I'm just happy to get out of this house and spend some time with him. It feels so good to be free." I twirled around my room with my arms out until an alert dinged on my phone.

A text from Drew scrolled across the lock screen. *I'm here. You ready?* 😊

A ridiculous smile spread across my face.

"Look at her! I'd say he's here," Shelby said.

I nodded and stared at myself in the mirror. I ventured somewhat from my comfort zone with a tank top, but even Shelby couldn't convince me from wearing my white sneakers.

"Sophie, Drew is here!" Mama called from the hallway.

"Be right there."

I hugged Riley and Shelby. "Thank you. I don't know where'd I be without the two of you."

"We love you too," Riley said.

Shelby nudged me to the door. "Now go, and text us when you get back. We want all the details, especially me. I have to live vicariously through you."

I rolled my eyes and giggled. "Bye."

Mama waited by the front door as she watched out the window. She clapped as she saw me walk out. "You look beautiful." She embraced me then pulled me back a tad to look into my gaze. "If you need anything, call me, and I'll come get you."

I eyed her warily. "It's Drew, Mama. You and I both know he isn't like that."

She shrugged. "I know, but I want you to know I'm on your side. No matter what."

I smiled and squeezed her hand. "I love you."

"I love you too."

I opened the door, and my jaw slackened.

Drew's hair was flatter to his head. He wore dark brown khaki pants and a pale blue T-shirt underneath an open short-sleeved, button up pink and white plaid shirt. He hands down looked more handsome than ever before. "Wow."

Drew looked around then back at me. "What?"

"You. You look so handsome."

Drew's cheeks reddened, and he adjusted his glasses. "You're the beautiful one."

"Thank you."

Drew reached for my hand, and I grabbed it. We walked hand in hand as he directed us to the passenger side of his car. He opened the door and waited until I climbed in before he closed it. Then he walked around to get in himself.

I slid my hands over my legs, willing the nervous energy to dissipate. This night was a big deal, and every cell of my being could sense that.

"I'm so happy we're doing this," Drew said.

I smiled and glanced at him. "Me too. It's still so surreal though."

Drew nodded. "Well worth the wait."

I grinned and kept an eye on the road, trying to figure out where we were headed. The ride to town was short, and I was surprised when we stopped by the park.

Drew stepped out and walked to my side to open the door. "Madam."

I giggled. "You're being silly."

Drew feigned hurt. "Me, silly? Never. I'm being a gentleman."

"That you are."

Drew linked his arm with mine and led us toward the middle of the park. "Where are we going?"

"Well, first I thought we could let you absorb the sun, yanno, since you're a runner."

I gasped and swatted at his arm.

Drew chuckled. "But no, really, I have a spot I wanted us to visit."

My eyebrow rose. What could be in the park that was important to see?

We walked in what felt like a random direction while I soaked in the warmth. The days had warmed since entering May. I loved the springtime and the days getting longer and warmer. It was one of my favorite seasons in Honey Cove.

Drew stopped suddenly, and I nearly ran into him.

I looked around where we were. As far as I could tell, this was just a part of the park. What did I need to see? A few birds were perched in the tree nearby, and a couple were walking on the outer path.

Drew faced me and grabbed both of my hands and held them in front of us. "Do you recognize where we are standing?"

"In the park?"

Drew chuckled. "Yes, but do you recognize the spot?"

I surveyed the area again, but no matter what, it just looked like a part of the park. "I don't think so."

"This is the spot where I knew I couldn't hide my feelings for you anymore." He smiled at my confusion. "It's where the bracelet table was."

"Right here?"

He nodded. "When I saw you eyeing the bracelets and the glint in your eye, it just felt right to buy it for you, and that's when I realized I never stopped having feelings for you. It's different with us being older, but it's certainly strong."

I smiled. "That's so sweet, Drew." I sighed. "Why are you so patient with me?"

Drew stroked my hair. "You forget that I've seen you at your lighter moments. Why wouldn't I wait for that? Or help you get there again?"

I leaned into his hand and covered it with mine. "You're so wonderful to me."

"You're pretty wonderful yourself. I mean, look at that smile. How could you not feel better from that?"

My cheeks reddened. "I don't know about that."

Drew tilted my chin up. "Don't do that. You are so wonderful. You must remember that yourself."

"Well, thank you. Maybe one day I can."

Drew smiled. "Want to grab some food?"

I nodded.

We walked hand in hand to Drew's car then drove into town.

"Does Over Easy's work?"

I nodded.

Drew grinned and squeezed my hand.

~

The crowd was mild, leaving most seats open. Drew led us to a booth in the back and waited until I slid in before he sat.

His eyes gleamed more than I had ever seen. It was like the happiness just couldn't be contained and burst itself through. I couldn't take my eyes off him. His happiness drew me in like a moth to a flame. I just didn't understand how I could make someone so incandescently happy, but I didn't want to fight it anymore.

We ordered our meals and drinks and were left in silence.

"So … I wanted to ask you something."

I raised my eyebrow. "Is that so?"

He nodded. "I was hoping to wait a little longer, but the anticipation is killing me."

I wiggled in the booth to lean closer to the table. "Okay."

"I know this is our first real date, but, Sophie, I don't need

more dates to know how I feel about you. Would you …
would you be my girlfriend?"

"Your girlfriend?"

He nodded.

"I think I could manage that."

Drew grinned. "Yeah? You mean it?"

"I like you a lot too, Drew. You make me feel things I
didn't know were possible. I don't want to separate from that
anymore. You make me feel renewed, as if connections can
conquer everything. The energy is all around us."

Drew leaned forward and grabbed my hand. "You make
me glad to be here and with you every day." He kissed my
hand then used it to pull me closer.

His face was merely inches from me.

I closed my eyes, and his lips found mine. His lips were
soft and tender. He didn't push, he didn't try and consume,
he just comforted as gently as possible. It made my heart sing
in a way I thought was only for other girls.

I'm not sure how I ended up someone who believed in
having a boyfriend. Or wasn't so cynical about love. But I
was sure glad for the outcome because I could have never
imagined it would feel like this.

ACKNOWLEDGMENTS

It is strange to write this page on my fourth novel. As was true with the others, this book would not have been possible without the help of many people. First, I want to thank my publisher Creative James Media for continuing to believe in my ideas.

I also want to thank Brian Paone for his wonderful editing services and advice. I am always learning how to be a better writer from his notes. Diana TC for her amazing cover work.

Alaine Greyson is my critique partner without whom I would be lost. She never tires of reading my drafts, no matter how many times she has seen it.

To my beta readers: KOBM, DM, Debra, Whitney, and Johanna. You all helped me immensely to make this book the way it is. I am grateful for the feedback and time you spent on this story.

Finally to my family for dealing with my craziness towards deadlines and encouraging me to take risks and follow my dreams.

Please consider leaving a review after reading.
Goodreads Review
Amazon Review

For the latest news and updates, please check out Marie McGrath on her social media pages. Exclusive content and sneak peeks can be found in her FB Fan Page.

Twitter: @Marie_McGrath_
Instagram: marie_mcgrath_
Facebook: www.facebook.com/MarieMcGrathAuthor
Facebook Fan Page: www.facebook.com/groups/MarieMcGrathFans
Website: https://mariemcgrathauthor.wixsite.com/books
Newsletter: https://mailchi.mp/a07cddcef872/marie-mcgrath-fans

ABOUT THE AUTHOR

Marie McGrath lives in a small rural town in Maryland. She hopes to inspire others with her stories. Her favorite genres to read are YA Romance and Contemporary Fiction. She loves the color turquoise, lions, and listening to music.